ACK WATER CANYON

W .e. ugene MaCCarthy attempts to take
c' ... e ranches and land around Santa
... lew Mexico, in his move to rule the
... y, he enlists the aid of the Hart gang
... their abortive raid on a bank in
C ... do. Arson, rustling and double-cross
f(... in quick succession, with suspicion
tl ... on Frank McCoy, owner of the Lazy
A ... s attempt to clear himself, the
d ... ry of gold in Black Water Canyon
a ... e unmasking of Eugene MaCCarthy
n ... an exciting, fast-moving tale of the
V ...

BLACK WATER CANYON

BLACK WATER CANYON

by

Jim Bowden

Dales Large Print Books
Long Preston, North Yorkshire,
BD23 4ND, England.

British Library Cataloguing in Publication Data.

Bowden, Jim
    Black Water Canyon

    A catalogue record of this book is
    available from the British Library

    ISBN   978-1-84262-704-4 pbk

First published in Great Britain in 1963 by Robert Hale Ltd.

Copyright © Jim Bowden 1963

Cover illustration © Gordon Crabb by arrangement with
Alison Eldred

The moral right of the author has been asserted

Published in Large Print 2010 by arrangement with
Mr W. D. Spence

Dales Large Print is an imprint of Library Magna Books Ltd.

Printed and bound in Great Britain by
T.J. (International) Ltd., Cornwall, PL28 8RW

Chapter One

'Wal, Clint, I guess I'll be goin'.' Dan McCoy, tall, slim, Sheriff of Red Springs, pushed himself from his chair. 'If there's any trouble tonight you know where to find me; Barbara and I will be at the Parkers.'

Clint Schofield, leather-faced, deputy-sheriff, who looked ten years less than his fifty-three, nodded. 'Sure, Dan,' he said and watched the young sheriff cross the office to the door. Clint admired the young man and thought how proud Dan's father would have been of his son. Clint settled himself in his chair to read the local paper. All was quiet in Red Springs and the deputy-sheriff did not anticipate any trouble apart from the odd drunk.

An hour passed before Clint was startled by a shot. He dropped his paper and leaped to his feet realising that he must have dozed off. He grabbed his Stetson, ran from the office and headed for the saloon from where he reckoned the shot had come. With gun in hand he burst through the batwings to halt in his tracks when he saw a man, holding a Colt, standing over a body sprawling on the floor.

'Drop it!' barked Clint sharply.

The gun slipped slowly from the man's fingers and clattered on the wooden boards. Slowly the man turned round to face his challenger.

Clint gasped with surprise when the light fell full on the man's face.

'Zeke Dolan!'

The man stared at the lawman through half-closed eyes. Slowly they widened with surprise.

'Clint Schofield!' he yelled, stepping forward, only to halt suddenly when Clint's Colt motioned to him.

'Hold it, Zeke,' warned Clint, his sense of duty as a lawman overcoming his pleasure in seeing an old friend. 'What's happened? Did you kill that man?'

Zeke nodded dejectedly. 'Yeah,' he admitted. 'But it was in self-defence.'

Cowboys along the bar grunted their approval.

'Sure is right,' offered the bar-tender. 'The cowpoke riled this old-timer until he could take no more. He told the cowpoke to cut it out but he wouldn't. Zeke was pressed hard so he pushed the youngster away. He went fer his gun but the old-timer was quicker. The cowpoke sure hed it comin' to him.'

Murmers of agreement with the story went round the saloon.

Clint nodded to two men who stepped forward to remove the body. The deputy sheriff picked up Zeke's gun and handed it back to him.

'Sure, glad I haven't to arrest you,' he said with a grin, slipping his own Colt back into its holster. 'Now, what you havin' to drink?'

A grin spread over Zeke's face as he stepped forward slapping Clint on the back.

'I'm shore glad to see you again,' he said. 'Didn't know you'd returned to Red Springs.'

Clint called for the drinks and looked hard at his friend. He was about Clint's age and looked it. The days spent in the open had beaten and chiseled his face but Clint noticed that his blue eyes still held the sparkle, and zest for life they had had when he had last seen Zeke. His clothes were worn and dusty and his battered sombrero lay on the bar.

'I came back here, after our last trip into the mountains, ten years ago,' explained Clint. 'I became deputy to Walt McCoy; he was gunned down about three years back an' now I'm deputy to his son. Never had the urge to look fer gold since. I suppose it's never left you.'

Zeke grinned. 'Darned right it hasn't,' he said. 'I guess I'll go on lookin' 'til the end of my days.' He sipped his whiskey, his eyes staring unseeingly in front of him as if he was trying to recapture something of the past. 'Remember that mine near Thunder Mountain up in Idaho?' he went on.

'You're goin' back some,' said Clint, 'but I sure do. You saved my life up there – remember that landslide?'

Zeke nodded and grinned. 'Then there were the two gals in Tuscarora, thought we'd come out of the mountain with a packet.'

Clint started to chuckle. 'Yeah, we got out of there pretty quick when they found out we had nothin'.' He laughed and drained his glass. He looked at Zeke.

'An' you've never struck it rich?'

Zeke shook his head and smiled. 'Nope,' he replied. 'But I've no regrets; it's been a good life; still is an' you never know what's in the next place you look.'

'Wal, you won't find gold around here,' said Clint.

'I know that,' answered Zeke. 'I'm jest passin' through; headin' fer New Mexico.' He paused and looked at Clint with a twinkle in his eye. 'How about comin' with me, Clint? It'd jest be like old times.'

Clint looked startled. 'What! Come to...' he stopped; his eyes widened as he saw a grin cross Zeke's face. 'You haven't another sure thing, hev you?'

Dolan's eyes gleamed. He looked round the room before leaning closer to his friend. 'A map,' he whispered, 'map of a lost mine in the mountains near Santa Rosa. Interested?'

'Wal,' drawled Clint trying not to appear too enthusiastic, although the meeting with his one time partner and the talk of old-times had revived memories of gold. 'I'm always interested in such things but that's not to say I'll come with you.'

'I'll show you the map, an' see what you think to it,' said Zeke, 'but not here. Can we go over to your office?'

'Sure,' replied Clint.

The two friends left the saloon and a few minutes later Zeke was spreading a map on the sheriff's desk.

'Look at this, Clint,' said Zeke excitedly, his eyes gleaming as he looked at the few ink markings which made up the map. 'There's gold there; right there in Black Water Canyon,' he added stabbing the map with

11

his finger.

The lawman leaned forward examining the map carefully. 'Where did you git this?' he asked, a note of eagerness in his voice.

'An old friend of mine in Austin was dying,' explained Zeke. 'I'd done him a favour about five years ago an' he felt he was repayin' me when he gave me this jest before he died. He assured me there was gold in the mountains of New Mexico and signalled out Black Water Canyon as the place to find it.' He paused a moment watching Clint who was eagerly tracing positions and distances on the map.

'Seems a lot here to indicate its accuracy,' said Clint half to himself, 'but as fer gold...'

'How about it, Clint? Let's go in this together,' suggested Zeke enthusiastically.

'But you're goin' it alone,' said Clint. 'You wouldn't want to share this with anyone.'

'Of course I would,' replied Dolan, 'especially with an old friend; somebody to talk to on the trail; somebody to share the thrill of finding gold. C'm on! What d'you say, Clint?'

Clint looked thoughtfully at the map. He shook his head. 'Mm ... no ... I'm too old for it now ... too old.'

'You're not,' replied Zeke eagerly. 'You're never too old to look fer gold. You'd do better

12

than many a youngster. We've been partners before, an' this is no shot in the dark.'

'We aren't certain it's genuine,' pointed out Clint.

'I know we've had maps before, but this one ... somehow it's different,' answered Zeke. 'There's only one way to find out if it's genuine. C'm on, jest one more try. It'll be a bonanza this time.'

'Ten years is a long time to be out of prospectin',' said Clint. 'I'm a lawman now; I can't run out on Dan.'

'You wouldn't be runnin' out,' answered Zeke. 'You'd be comin' back.'

'Wal...' Seeing Clint's hesitation, Zeke seized his chance and pressed the matter.

'Jest think of those nights round a camp fire, hot coffee under the stars,' said Zeke, 'those vast mountains rising to the heavens, the wind sighing in the pines, there's nothing like it, Clint, on the trail looking for gold.'

Zeke could see Clint was weakening. He had a faraway look in his eye. Thoughts of those past days with his friend, the comradeship that had grown up between them. It would be good to be with him on the trail again. The desire to look for gold was stirring in Clint. He knew that gold fever in men could be a terrible thing, and they

13

would go to no ends to get it, but he also knew it had never been like that with them. The lust for gold had never firmly gripped them. It would be just the same now and even if they found nothing they would count it a gain to have been together once more.

Clint rubbed his chin thoughtfully. 'It might be our last chance together,' he muttered.

'It might,' pressed Zeke. 'What about it?'

Suddenly Clint turned sharply to face his friend. He brought his fist hard down on the table. 'By golly, I'll go,' he shouted.

'Good man,' yelled Zeke excitedly as he gripped Clint firmly by the hand, and clapped him on the back.

'Dan isn't goin' to like this,' said Clint. He paused thoughtfully, rubbing his chin. 'Maybe he won't take it so badly; I'll be able to contact his brother Frank, who has a ranch near Santa Rosa. Look, Zeke, I can't git hold of Dan now, he's out for the evenin', but he'll be home about eleven. We'll hev to leave it until the morning.'

'But I've got all planned for an early start,' said Zeke. 'We'll go an' see him at eleven.'

'All right,' agreed Clint, and the two men spent the rest of the night yarning.

At eleven o'clock Clint locked the office

and the two men made their way to the house occupied by the McCoys. A light shone from one of the windows and Clint's knock was answered by Dan.

'Hello, Clint,' he greeted. 'Come in.'

As the door closed behind them Clint turned to Dan. 'I'd like you to meet an old friend, Zeke Dolan.'

Dan extended his hand and gripped Zeke's firmly. 'Pleased to meet you,' he said. He led the way into a room where he offered the two men a seat.

'Thought I heard a shot come over this evening,' he went on. 'Had any trouble?'

'Zeke shot some drifter,' answered Clint. Noting Dan's surprised look he hastened to add, 'Self defence an' there were plenty of witnesses.'

The door opened and Dan's pretty wife Barbara came in to greet the two men pleasantly. 'Thought I heard Clint's voice,' she said, 'so I've put some coffee on, I knew he wouldn't say no to a cup.'

'Thanks, Barbara,' returned Clint. 'You see how spoilt I am, Zeke; it makes things all the harder.' He looked sheepishly at Dan and his wife. Suddenly he blurted out. 'Dan, I may as well come straight to the point; I've decided to go to New Mexico with Zeke.'

Dan and Barbara stared incredulously at the deputy.

'But what for?' gasped Dan.

'Gold!' answered Clint eagerly. 'Zeke has a map an' I feel I've got to go jest once more.'

'But Clint, what about your job here? I need you,' said Dan.

'I'll be back,' answered Clint. 'Jack or Howard can help you out until then. Besides, I'll be able to take all your news to Frank.'

Dan smiled. 'I know,' he said, 'but don't forget it's ten years since you had this urge an' the trails in New Mexico can be pretty rugged; it can be hard on you, Clint. Why not leave it at your time of life? Both of you forget it. Zeke, why not settle down here? I've just got a ranch an' I could use you.'

'Thanks, Dan. I know you mean well,' replied Zeke, 'but I've been driftin' and prospectin' all my life. I'd feel cooped up in a bunk-house; I wouldn't settle. My only roof has been God's stars, an' I guess they will be 'till the end of my days. If I find gold, then, I find it, an' if I don't, I'll be jest as happy 'cos there's more riches an' more beauty in what I see as I drift along than there is in all the gold mines in the country.'

Dan smiled. 'Wal, I'm glad it's not gold fever that's got you, an' I can understand the

16

way you feel, but if ever you feel the trails are too much for you come back here.'

'That's mighty nice of you,' said Zeke. 'I'll sure remember your offer.'

Dan looked at Clint. He knew that with Zeke there the urge to have another look at the old life was strong. 'You know, Clint,' he said, 'I'll rely a lot more on you when we get this ranch fixed up an' especially when we move in there; not that I'll neglect my duties as sheriff but you know how it will be.'

Clint nodded but said nothing.

Barbara looked kindly at the older man who had been almost a second father to her husband. 'That coffee will be ready now so I'll suggest that you sleep on the decision tonight but don't forget that you'll find the trails harder than they were. Now come on and enjoy the coffee and a smoke.'

An hour later the two old friends left McCoy's. They walked down the street to the hotel. Zeke looked at the building disgusted when they stopped outside.

'How I hate these places,' he shuddered. 'But what can you do when you're in town. However it's only for one night. I'll be away early in the mornin', probably before you'll see McCoy, so what about it, Clint?'

Clint looked doubtful.

'Jest one more try,' whispered Zeke, 'jest fer old times sake.'

Clint hesitated, uncertain what to do. 'All right,' he replied suddenly. An excitement showed in his eyes as he made the decision.

'Good man!' Zeke was equally as excited to have his old partner on the trail with him. 'Meet me here at sun-up.'

Clint nodded and bade his friend goodnight. He walked slowly to the sheriff's office where he lit the lamp and sat down behind the desk. He picked up a sheet of paper and a pen and wrote a brief note of explanation to Dan. When he had signed his name and laid down his pen he unpinned the star from his shirt and placed it on top of the letter. He sat for a few moments staring at it, his mind flooding with the memories of a life he had thought would be his until his dying day.

Suddenly he started, stood up, blew out the lamp and hurried from the office leaving the moonlight to pick out the solitary tin star lying on Dan's desk.

Chapter Two

Tom Price and Kit Sheridan, owners of the Running W and Circle J, sat at a table in the Ace of Spades, a bottle of whiskey between them. Both were in their early thirties and five years earlier had come to New Mexico together to buy land near Santa Rosa and start ranching.

'I reckon these rumours should be looked into,' said the burly, dark-haired Tom Price. 'It's in the interests of all the ranchers around Santa Rosa.'

Sheridan drained his glass and nodded. He looked thoughtful as he stroked his moustache with his thumb and forefinger and poured himself another drink.

'It's about time we ranchers formed our-selves into a protective association,' he said. 'It's an idea I've had for some time, but it seems to me thet it's becomin' more important now thet someone's buyin' land all around us.'

'Thet's if these rumours are true,' pointed out Price.

'Wal, if they are,' said Sheridan, 'whoever's buyin' the land can do us a lot of harm. I've heard of these syndicates buying up land an' forcing the local ranchers out of business. It's high time we looked into this before it goes too far.'

'I've heard Floyd Wheeler's name linked with the deals,' said Price as he refilled his glass.

'Floyd Wheeler! Hardly likely,' laughed Sheridan.

'Oh, I don't know,' replied Price seriously. 'He'd hev plenty of money from the Ace of Spades, an' if he wasn't buyin' fer himself then he would be actin' fer someone else.'

'Wal, there's only one way to find out,' said Sheridan. 'Let's ask him.'

Price laughed scornfully. 'Do you think he'd tell us?' He drained his glass and pushed himself to his feet, swaying a little as he did so. 'C'm on,' he said. 'I've a better idea, we'll go over to the bank an' ask Grove Farrell, then if it is Wheeler he won't know that we're on to him.'

Sheridan grunted, picked up his Stetson and climbed to his feet eyeing his companion doubtfully as he saw him lurch away from the table.

The two men crossed the floor and left the

Ace of Spades. Tom Price swung his bulky frame round the post at the end of the rails opposite the door and stepped down into the dust of Main Street. He took one step forward and pulled up so sharply that Kit Sheridan bumped into him.

'What the...' snapped the thin-faced, moustached owner of the Circle J.

'Look,' returned Price. His voice had a tone of urgency in it as he nodded towards the bank. 'That's the land grabbin' coyote,' he snarled angrily.

Sheridan followed Tom's gaze and saw Floyd Wheeler, smartly dressed in tailed-coat and neatly-creased matching trousers, closing the door of the bank behind him. He paused, took a watch from the pocket of his fancy, pearl-buttoned waistcoat and glanced at the time. Tall, slim with dark hair brushed neatly back and a thin, short trimmed moustache Wheeler cut a smart figure as he turned and walked along the sidewalk.

Price grunted. 'I'll kill the land grabbin'...' he hissed between tight lips.

He lurched forward but Kit Sheridan grabbed his arm pulling him up short. Price turned sharply glaring angrily at his friend.

'Shut up,' snapped Sheridan harshly. 'You've no proof; you'll find yourself at the end of a rope if you go on like that. You've had too much whiskey.'

Price pulled hard trying to free his arm but Sheridan held on firmly.

'Gun-play with Wheeler won't solve anythin',' went on Sheridan. His voice was low but urgent. 'He may not be buyin' land an' even if he is, it's no crime.'

He saw the anger dying in Price's eyes and when he noticed Wheeler turn the corner, near the stage office, he released his grip on his friend.

'Sorry, Kit,' mumbled Price apologetically. 'I guess seeing Wheeler just riled me when I thought of what he might be doin'. C'm on, we'll go an' see what we can learn at the bank.'

Sheridan was about to try to dissuade Price from going but he was as curious himself. 'All right,' he said, 'but watch that temper of yours.'

The two men crossed the street and walked along the sidewalk to the bank. Opening the door they stepped inside to find the two bank clerks dealing with two customers, whilst a third man waited his turn. One of the clerks looked up when Price and Sheridan entered and, when Sheridan pointed to a door at the end of the room, he nodded indicating that the manager was in. The two ranchers crossed to the door and, receiving a call of 'Come in,' to their knock, they entered the office.

'Good day, gentlemen,' greeted the man behind the huge leather-topped mahogany desk. 'What can I do for you?' He indicated two chairs and the two men sat down.

'Howdy, Farrell,' said Price eyeing the man behind the desk with interest. He saw a neatly-turned out man of fifty whose greying hairs added a distinguished look to what had once been a handsome face. But it was the eyes which Price disliked. 'If it wasn't for Farrell's eyes he would be a likeable man,' he had always said, and now he found himself again fascinated by the eyes, which looked cold even though the face was broken with a smile. 'Shifty in a cunning way,' thought Price. 'I wouldn't trust him if...' his thoughts were interrupted by Sheridan who was speaking.

'We would like some information an' we think you might be able to help us. We have heard rumours that a great deal of land is being bought up in the neighbourhood of our ranches, an' we thought you might be able to tell us who is buyin' it.'

Grove Farrell looked from one man to the

other before speaking. 'Really, gentlemen.' His voice sounded as if he was disgusted. 'If this were true do you think I would betray a customer's confidence. I am a bank manager and...'

'You get a lot of information,' broke in Price hastily. 'If one man is buyin' all this land it could mean ruin for us if he so wished.'

Farrell turned his eyes on Price. 'Rumours, you said they were rumours,' he said smoothly. 'Gentlemen, you shouldn't believe all the rumours you hear.'

The smooth, gloating tone in his voice, as if he took pleasure in knowing something that others didn't know, coupled with the contemptuous look in his eyes angered Price. He jumped to his feet.

'Who's buyin' that land?' he shouted. 'Is it Wheeler?'

Farrell looked up at the man leaning over his desk. 'Please, Mister Price, let us be sensible about this. If anyone is doing what you say, and I knew, I am afraid I could not tell you.'

Price's lips tightened. 'I'll get you an'...'

A wry smile flicked Farrell's lips as he leaned back in his chair but his eyes were cold and penetrating. 'Don't threaten me,

Price,' he snapped whip like. 'You are in no position to do so. There could be a little matter of some borrowed money being called in by the bank.'

'Why you…' stormed Price angrily.

Sheridan jumped from his chair and gripped his friend by the shoulders.

'Steady, Tom,' he said firmly. 'We'll learn nothin' here. I'm afraid Farrell is too eager to throw our overdrafts in our faces. C'm on let's go.'

'Sensible man, Mister Sheridan,' praised the bank manager mockingly. 'Good day, gentlemen,' he added, finalising the interview. He bent over his desk and proceeded to examine some papers as if Price and Sheridan were not there.

Price glared angrily at the bank manager but Sheridan turned him firmly away from the desk.

As the door closed behind them Grove Farrell looked up, sneered contemptuously, pursed his lips thoughtfully and chuckled to himself.

Stepping out into the hot afternoon sun Tom Price and Kit Sheridan paused on the sidewalk. Floyd Wheeler walked along the boards on the opposite side of the road towards the Ace of Spades.

'C'm on,' said Price. 'We'll ask the man himself.'

'What's the use,' said Sheridan restraining his friend. 'You said yourself it wouldn't be any good approaching Wheeler. Let's ride home,' he added, hoping to get Price away from town.

Price shook himself free and stepped off the sidewalk. 'I'm goin' to see Wheeler,' he called over his shoulder. 'Coming?'

Kit watched his friend cross the street before he moved, then, a decision made, he ran after Tom and caught up to him just before he reached the Ace of Spades. He could not leave Price in his present frame of mind to approach Wheeler alone; he must stay with him to see he reached the Running W safely.

They hurried into the saloon and saw Floyd Wheeler climbing the stairs to enter a room half way along the balcony above the bar. The two men followed Wheeler and when they stepped inside the room they found Wheeler seated behind a large table manicuring his nails. His hands were long and supple with no sign of hard, manual work upon them. His smart, elegant appearance belied a quick brain and a strong firm personality, two attributes which he often played down for his own ends. A broad-shouldered, square-jawed cowboy lounged in a chair at one side of the desk. Price and Sheridan glanced sharply at each other wondering if this was an opportune moment to approach Wheeler with Butch Lant in the room. Butch was known to be Wheeler's law-and-order man.

'Well, boys, what can I do fer you?' asked Wheeler glancing at the two ranchers as they entered the room.

Neither man spoke for a moment then Price, realising they would gain nothing by showing weakness moved his burly frame forward.

'Wheeler,' he said sharply, 'we hear that you've been buyin' a lot of land, we want to know if it's true an' if so what your intentions are.'

Price was looking straight at the owner of the Ace of Spades but Sheridan, who stood a little behind his friend, noticed that Lant was startled by Price's bluntness and eased himself into a more upright position moving his hand a little nearer his holster.

A grin spread across Wheeler's face. 'What would I want with land?' he said softly.

'Thet's what we want to know,' snapped Price before Wheeler could say any more.

The smile slowly vanished from Wheeler's face and his lips tightened in a thin, determined line. 'Manners, Price, manners,' he hissed. 'You come in here demanding to know my business and you're not very pleasant about it. Whether what you say is true or not you'd be better minding your own affairs.'

His eyes narrowed looking hard at the two men in front of him.

Price glared angrily at Wheeler. His hand moved swiftly towards his side, but before he could draw his gun, a cold, quiet voice stopped him.

'Hold it!'

The rancher glanced sideways and saw the cold muzzle of a Colt pointing at him.

'Don't threaten Mister Wheeler,' went on Butch Lant slowly. 'If you know what's good fer you you'll walk right out of here now, an' fergit the whole thing.'

The two men hesitated then looked sharply at Wheeler who grinned back at them.

'Good day, gentlemen,' he said quietly and returned his attention to his finger nails.

The two ranchers turned and walked from the room. Kit could sense that Tom was fuming with rage at the treatment he had received but he was not prepared for the

28

fury of Tom's tongue as they walked down the stairs.

'Why the hell didn't you back me up?' snarled Price.

'I knew it would be useless as soon as I saw Lant,' explained Sheridan. 'I don't want any gun-play with a hired-gun either,' he added.

'We could hev got the drop on them,' snapped Price, 'an' then made them talk.'

'I think you're over estimatin' yourself,' answered Sheridan sharply.

'Like hell I am,' rapped Price. 'I'll show thet fancy clothes some day that he can't push Tom Price around.'

'All right,' said Sheridan as they passed through the doorway on to the sidewalk. 'Now let's calm down an' git back home.'

The two friends whose ranch-houses were only a mile apart rode back together but noting that Tom was still moody Sheridan said nothing. As they were parting Price looked anxiously at his friend.

'Wal, do you think Wheeler's behind these rumours?' he asked.

'It's hard to tell,' answered Sheridan thoughtfully rubbing his moustache. 'Lant was startled when you brought up the subject an' Wheeler didn't deny it; in fact I've been thinking over what he said an' my impression is that maybe he knows more than he cares to say.'

Price grunted. 'I'll say he knows a darned lot.'

'Then I'm all fer gettin' a protective association formed,' said Sheridan urgently. 'If the big owners like Frank McCoy an' Mark Stevens will come in we'll be on a strong footing.'

'Right,' agreed Price. 'Tomorrow morning we'll see what they all say.'

It was noon when Frank McCoy, tall, slim, fair-haired owner of the Lazy A slid from his horse in front of the ranch-house. He tied the horse to the rail and went inside the house where his pretty, dark-haired wife Abigail ran to meet him. He kissed her lightly on the lips and with his arm round her waist went into the dining-room.

'All go well this morning?' asked Abigail.

'Yes,' replied Frank flopping wearily into a chair. 'Most of the branding's done an' we hev over a hundred head of new cattle.'

'Good,' said Abigail. 'Dinner is almost ready. It will be on the table by the time you've washed that dust off.'

Frank and Abigail were sitting down to the meal when the pound of hooves attracted their attention.

'More than two or three riders comin',' observed Frank. 'Hope nothin's gone wrong on the range.' He looked anxious as he hurried on to the verandah followed by his wife.

Six riders approached at a steady pace.

'Mark, Tom Price, Kit Sheridan, Abe Carson, Wes Briton, Luke Martin and George Hardy,' whispered Abigail as she studied the riders.

'We've got all the ranch owners in the neighbourhood, Abbe,' said Frank. 'Somethin' must be troublin' them.'

'Guess I'd better keep the dinner warm,' remarked Abbe and went back into the house.

The riders pulled to a halt in front of the ranch-house and greeted Frank pleasantly.

Frank nodded a welcome to each rider. 'Now, you aren't out ridin' for the good of your health so you'd better come inside an' tell me what's eatin' you.'

The men slipped from the saddles and tied their horses to the rail.

'How are you settlin' down after your honeymoon, Mark?' asked Frank as they walked into the house.

Mark grinned. 'Things are goin' fine,' he replied. 'Best day's work I ever did was when

I decided to act as foreman for Gloria Linden when her father was killed.'

'Good. I'm glad things worked out as they did,' said Frank.

'Bring Barbara over to see us some evening soon,' invited Mark.

'Wal, gentlemen,' said Frank as he closed the door when all the ranchers had entered the room. 'You're all lookin' mighty serious. What's troublin' you?'

They all looked at Kit, who, it appeared, had been elected spokesman.

'Frank, we're all worried about the rumours that are flyin' around about the purchase of land around Santa Rosa,' he said.

Frank pursed his lips thoughtfully. 'What rumours hev you heard?' he asked.

'Don't tell us you hevn't heard them?' snapped Price irritably.

Frank looked at him sharply. 'I've heard certain things,' he answered testily, 'but then I don't pay much attention to rumours. Maybe you gentlemen would be wiser to do the same; unless you've got somethin' more to go on.'

'Wal,' went on Sheridan. 'Some of us hev heard thet Floyd Wheeler is doin' all the buyin' an'...'

'Floyd Wheeler!' interrupted Frank with a

laugh. 'Never, Floyd.'

'Why not?' asked Wes Briton sharply.

'Wal, could you imagine Wheeler goin' in fer land an' cattle; he's strictly a town man,' replied Frank.

'How do you know?' queried Luke Martin.

'Look here, Luke,' said Frank firmly, 'When Abbe's father was murdered an' the whole affair cleared up we decided to sell the Ace of Spades, we couldn't run both the saloon an' the ranch and we preferred the ranch. In his time Abbe's father did a lot fer Santa Rosa an' tried to keep out property grabbin' folk so when we were sellin' we decided to be most careful whom we chose. Ever heard of Doane Rogers?'

There were murmurs of recognition as Frank paused.

'Biggest gambler an' saloon owner in Texas,' said Mark.

Frank nodded. 'An' I'll tell you now, thet we could hev hed half as much again fer the Ace of Spades if we'd sold out to him. But you know what would hev happened in Santa Rosa once Rogers had got a foothold.' Frank paused to let his words sink in. 'We sold to Wheeler because we thought he seemed straight enough. There's never been any complaints about the way he runs

33

things, has there?'

'No,' agreed Sheridan, 'there hasn't, but there are these rumours about this land buyin'.'

'Wal, he may have the money,' replied Frank, 'but I can't see Wheeler buyin' it fer himself.'

'Now there's a point,' said Abe Carson. 'He may not be buyin' it fer himself but he could be a cover for someone else.'

'Wal, I think they're jest a lot of rumours,' said Frank. 'Someone's seen or heard somethin'; put two an' two together an' made five. Hev you any proof; anythin' to work on?'

'Kit an' I paid a visit to Grove Farrell an' Floyd Wheeler yesterday,' put in Tom Price. 'We challenged them both about the rumours.'

'Learn anythin'?' asked Frank.

Price shook his head. 'No, Farrell wouldn't cooperate and Wheeler denied it.'

'Wal there you are,' said Frank shrugging his shoulders.

'Yeah, but I think Farrell knew somethin', an' Wheeler was certainly cagey,' replied Price.

'He hed that gunman with him,' said Sheridan in support of Price, 'an' I noticed he was all attention as soon as Tom questioned Wheeler.'

'But without proof we can do nothin',' said Frank. 'Best thing is to fergit the whole thing. No one person could buy up all the land they say has been bought.'

'Frank,' said Luke Martin, 'do you realise if this land has been bought then it is goin' to put us all in an awkward position. We would all be forced out; we little spreads couldn't face the pressure that could be brought to bear on us, you an' Mark with the bigger ranches might survive for some time. It can be serious, Frank, thet's why we'd like to see some sort of protective association formed.'

'Protective association by all means,' agreed Frank, 'but only if it is necessary, and I don't think thet has been proved yet.'

'But why wait, let's get together now,' argued Price. 'If whoever's buyin' the land sees we mean business then he'll be careful how far he goes.'

'All this means is, that you're pushing forward a split into two camps,' pointed out Frank, 'an' if you aren't careful we'll hev another Lincoln County War on our hands, an' you know what thet left in its wake, gunslingers, rustlers, murderers, Billy the Kid; we want no more of thet here. I'm all against an association unless it's absolutely necessary.'

'But unless we take action now,' shouted Price, 'it may be too late.'

'Wait…' started Frank.

'It's no good unless we're all of a same mind,' interrupted Mark. 'Let's wait a little longer, an' in the meantime see if we can find out any more about the rumours.'

'Good idea, Mark,' agreed one of the men and others called their approval.

'Wal,' said Sheridan, 'seems as if you don't approve of our idea but before long you'll all be wishing we'd formed this association today.'

Sheridan turned, flung open the door and hurried from the room followed quickly by Price. The remainder filed out of the house and, bidding Frank goodbye, they mounted their horses and rode away at a brisk trot. Price and Sheridan were some distance ahead of the others but when they were out of sight of the Lazy A they slowed down to allow the other ranchers to catch up with them.

'Hold hard,' called Price. 'Kit has some news which will interest you all.'

The riders pulled their mounts to a halt and looked curiously at Sheridan.

'What's wrong Kit?' asked Wes.

'Do you know who's bought Black Water Canyon an' its surroundin' land?' he asked.

'Sure,' replied Mark. 'Frank.'

The other cowboys nodded. 'Yeah, we know. What's wrong with thet?' called Abe.

'Seems curious to me,' put in Price quickly, 'thet he should buy at the same time as other land is being bought by an unknown buyer.'

'What you gettin' at?' asked Mark testily.

'Wal, couldn't McCoy be thet buyer,' pointed out Price.

'If he is then why didn't he keep the purchase of Black Water Canyon a secret?' asked Mark.

'A cover,' answered Price. 'To throw suspicion away from himself.'

A murmur ran through the group of riders when they realised what Tom Price was getting at.

'Hold hard,' called Mark angrily. 'First you accuse Wheeler; now it's Frank; who will it be next?'

'Couldn't they be workin' together,' pointed out Sheridan. 'Frank sold Wheeler the Ace of Spades so he got him up here an' now he could be gettin' Wheeler to do the buyin' for him. He's already got a big spread and by expandin' he could put us all in a funny position...'

'If he wanted to,' shouted Mark. 'An' thet's supposin' your theory's right which I don't believe for one moment thet it is.'

'We didn't expect you to,' snapped Price, 'you being such a close friend of McCoy.'

Mark stiffened, his eyes narrowing as he watched the burly rancher closely.

'We've got to explore all possibilities to protect ourselves,' pointed out Abe.

'Don't fergit McCoy was all against formin' a protective association; thet surprised me,' said Luke.

'I thought he'd hev been all fer it,' said another.

'He gave a good enough reason fer not formin' it,' called Mark.

'Maybe so but the Lincoln County War days were different an' we...'

'It could happen again,' snapped Mark.

'Wal, I think the whole set-up is suspicious an' I figure we ought to keep our eyes on Wheeler an' McCoy,' said Price. 'We'll all keep in close touch an' report immediately if anything suspicious happens. We'll git along without McCoy.'

'You in this, Mark?' asked Sheridan firmly.

All eyes turned on Mark Stevens as they waited for his reply.

He hesitated, thinking fast. 'I guess so,' he replied. 'If there is trouble ahead then we're better united. Mind you, I think you're wrong about Frank, an' if trouble blows up he'll be in to help us.'

'Maybe so,' answered Price testily, 'but I fer one will keep my eyes open where Frank McCoy is concerned!'

Chapter Three

As Frank watched his neighbours ride away he was troubled by their attitude. Deep in thought he walked back into the house where Abigail came out of the kitchen to meet him.

'Hope there's nothing wrong, darling,' she said as they went into the room.

'Not really,' replied Frank sitting down at the table. 'Rumours about this land buyin' appear to be flyin' thick and fast an' I'm afraid Tom Price an' Kit Sheridan hev been doin' some thinkin' which I hope is wrong.'

Abbe looked at Frank curiously. 'I never did like Tom Price,' she said, 'and I suppose Kit Sheridan sticks by him because they came out here together.'

Frank nodded. 'I can see their point,' he went on. 'Any of us could be swamped by someone on a large scale but their position is more precarious when they are operating only on a small scale. What really alarms me is thet they figure Floyd Wheeler is doin' all the buyin'.'

'What!' Abbe looked up in surprise.

'Makes things look a bit awkward fer us,' said Frank, 'seein' it was through us sellin' the Ace of Spades that he came here. But I believe it's someone bigger than Wheeler, maybe a syndicate from back east. I'm sure glad I bought Black Water Canyon as soon as I heard rumours of land buyin'; it strengthens our position a lot. The land around it is good grazin' ground so we can run a lot more cattle an' the Canyon can make a good holdin' place fer steers apart from givin' us an excellent additional water supply.'

'I'd like to come out there with you some time,' said Abbe.

'I was thinkin' of goin' in two or three days' time,' said Frank. 'We'll see what we can fix up.'

The conversation continued throughout the meal and Abigail was about to clear the table when the pound of a galloping horse brought questioning looks between husband and wife. They jumped to their feet and hurried to the verandah.

Mark Stevens pulled his sweating horse to a dust raising halt in front of his two friends.

'What's wrong, Mark?' asked Frank noting the worried look as his friend swung from the saddle and stepped on to the verandah.

'I've jest left the others,' explained Mark. 'Thought I'd better double back here an' warn you thet they're beginning to think you're behind all this land buying.'

'What!' Frank and Abbe gasped, looking at each other and then back at Mark in amazement.

'But why?' asked Abbe.

Mark went on to relate the theories of Tom Price. 'I thought I'd better warn you of the way men's minds work.'

'Thanks, Mark,' said Frank. He strode up and down thoughtfully for a moment before turning sharply to face his friend. 'You don't believe these ideas do you?' he asked anxiously.

'No, of course not,' protested Mark surprised that his friend should put such a question. 'But you must admit that when facts are twisted they can be made to tell any story.'

'I suppose so,' agreed Frank. 'An' what about this association?'

'Wal, I'm all fer showin' our strength by unity,' replied Mark, 'but I also think you've got a good point against it. But, the real reason for goin' along with them is so that we can know what they are doin' and thinkin'.'

'Nice work, Mark,' said Frank with a smile. 'A good idea and in the meantime I aim to try to find out more about this land buyin' myself.'

With dust billowing behind it, the stage-coach thundered into the main street of Santa Rosa. The driver pushed forcefully on the brake lever with his foot and hauled hard on the reins. The horses fought the pull of the leather and the locking of the wheels, but gradually the driver brought the coach to a slithering halt outside the office where the company's representative in Santa Rosa stood waiting to greet its arrival.

'All go well?' he asked as the shotgun jumped down on to the sidewalk.

'Sure,' replied the dust-covered man. 'No trouble at all.'

The official opened the door of the coach and greeted the occupants as they alighted. The first three being citizens of Santa Rosa were well known to him. They were greeted by their relatives who were among the small throng of people who had gathered on the sidewalk. The last traveller to leave the stage was a complete stranger to everyone and people stared curiously at him as he stepped from the coach.

He was tall, well dressed in a fawn frock-coat and neatly creased, matching trousers. His shoes were elegant and had obviously received recent treatment as they did not even show the dust of travel. He wore a fancy waistcoat and had a cravat neatly tied at his throat. His hair was greying at the temples adding a distinguished look to this man who was in his early fifties. As he stepped on to the sidewalk he placed a fawn top hat firmly on his head at just the right angle and turned to accept his valise which the driver of the stagecoach handed down to him.

'Thank you,' he said, 'and thank you for a good, smooth trip.'

He paused a moment, looking along the street and then, seeing the building for which he was looking, he stepped forward, bade his fellow passengers goodbye with a friendly smile, and strolled across the street to the hotel.

He booked the best room in the hotel,

ordered a bath to be run for him, and, when he had settled in, he enjoyed a meal before taking a closer look at Santa Rosa. It was a pleasant evening and he strolled slowly around the town noting its layout before making his way to the Ace of Spades. He took up a position at one end of the bar as he enjoyed his whiskey. The long, shining counter stretched almost the full length of the wall and at the opposite end of the room from where the stranger was standing was a stage. The floor was filled with tables but he noted that the gambling tables were at the end nearest to him. A staircase, with carved rails, led to the balcony which ran round three sides of the room. He passed his eyes slowly round the room, which was only just beginning to welcome its occupants for their night's entertainment, but did not see the man he sought. He was about to leave the bar when a door of a room off the balcony opened and Floyd Wheeler walked to the rail, stood for a minute or two looking at the scene below before returning to the room from which he had come. The stranger finished his drink, strolled between the gambling tables, studying the play for a few moments, before seating himself at a poker-table. He played carefully but all the time kept his eye on the door on the balcony.

Half an hour passed and no one had come out of the room. He finished the game and smiled at the other players.

'That's enough for me,' he said, 'so I'll bid you gentlemen goodnight.' He stood up, walked to the bar and called for a final whiskey and studied the balcony once again, making a note of a door which was in the wall at one end of the balcony.

He finished his drink and left the saloon. Keeping close to the wall he hurried round the building and found an outside wooden staircase leading to a door halfway up the wall. He glanced round and, seeing no one about, he climbed the stairs two at a time and gently tested the door. Finding it open he stepped inside to find himself, as he expected, on the balcony. He moved swiftly to the door which he had seen Wheeler use and his tap was answered by a loud 'Come in.'

'Good evening, Wheeler,' he greeted as he entered the room.

Wheeler, who was sitting in an easy chair, glanced up. A look of surprise crossed his face and he jumped to his feet.

'Welcome to Santa Rosa, Mister MacCarthy,' he said extending his hand and stepping forward to greet him. 'I didn't expect you for a few days. I'd have been at the stage to meet you.'

MacCarthy gripped Wheeler's hand firmly. 'I figured things were going well so I came early,' he said. He glanced at Butch Lant who lounged in another easy chair and Wheeler, seeing MacCarthy's look, turned to Lant who had been eyeing the newcomer curiously.

'Mister MacCarthy this is Butch Lant; Butch meet Mister Eugene MacCarthy.'

MacCarthy moved forward to shake hands but Lant merely nodded from his chair without rising.

MacCarthy's face hardened. He looked sharply at Wheeler, who felt uncomfortable at Lant's lack of respect.

'If you're going to continue to work for Floyd you'd better learn some manners,' snapped MacCarthy turning to Lant, 'an' if you're still going to earn your money you'd better remember that I call the tune.' Lant was so surprised at the venom and authority in the voice that he quickly pushed himself to his feet mumbling an apology. Mac-Carthy extended his hand again and this time Lant took it to be surprised once more by the firm powerful grip. 'Good,' smiled

46

MacCarthy. 'Now that we understand each other we'll get along all right together. Do your job well, Butch, and you'll find me a generous man.' He paused to let his words sink in. 'All right, now leave us; Floyd and I hev something to talk over.'

Lant nodded and hurried from the room. As the door closed behind him Wheeler started to apologise for the behaviour of his gun-man.

MacCarthy waved his hand. 'It's all right,' he said. 'I've experienced these rough types before. They don't go for these clothes, unless they know the man under them. Lant didn't know me, but now he understands who's the boss, and that this outfit covers a man of iron, he'll be all right, but I want to avoid using hired guns if possible.'

'Certainly,' said Wheeler. 'I hired Lant to keep order in the Ace of Spades and I thought he might be useful if any ranchers became stubborn over selling land...'

MacCarthy nodded and sat down. He accepted a cigar offered by Wheeler and when both men had lit them to their satisfaction MacCarthy spoke again.

'The purchasing of unowned land seems to have gone well; you've done a good job Floyd. I hope the bank manager is a discreet man, and that he has no idea who is behind the buying.'

Wheeler smiled. 'Grove Farrell is all right,' he said, 'but should he ever get awkward I have some information about him which could be very useful.'

A smile curled the corners of his lips and MacCarthy realised that, whilst he had a shrewd, useful ally, Floyd Wheeler was a man who had a nose for finding out the nasty side of a man's character, and would not hesitate to use that information should the necessity arise.

'Good,' said MacCarthy. 'What indiscretion has Farrell committed?'

'About ten years ago he pulled a quick, illegal deal and made himself a lot of money,' explained Wheeler.

MacCarthy nodded. 'Now what about the ranchers? Think they'll sell?'

Wheeler pursed his lips thoughtfully. 'Well, they're all men who hev made roots here and I think they'll present a problem.'

'Money talks, Wheeler,' replied MacCarthy. 'Make the price big enough and they'll sell.'

Wheeler looked doubtful. 'These ranchers can be a stubborn lot and if they unite they could be pretty powerful.'

'A chain is as strong as its weakest link,' reminded MacCarthy, 'and there'll be someone tempted by the cash and the rest could easily follow. Who owns the biggest spread?'

'Frank McCoy,' answered Wheeler. 'Boss of the Lazy A; used to be sheriff in Santa Rosa; married old man Clement's daughter; sold me the Ace of Spades. He beat me to the purchase of Black Water Canyon.'

'Mm,' grunted MacCarthy thoughtfully. 'Think he suspects anything?'

'I doubt it,' answered Wheeler. 'Natural expansion I should think.'

'Wal, if he proves difficult there are methods of persuasion,' grinned MacCarthy. He paused; the smile suddenly vanished and his voice became deadly serious. 'Of one thing I'm certain,' he said, 'I'm going to own and run this State and no one is going to stop me!'

'What's the first move?' asked Wheeler.

'Tomorrow you'll introduce me to Grove Farrell,' answered MacCarthy, 'and I'll arrange for offers to be sent to all the ranchers.'

It was a warm fine morning when Floyd Wheeler and Eugene MacCarthy crossed the street and entered the bank. Grove Farrell looked up as the two men entered his office.

'Good morning, Grove,' greeted Wheeler.

49

'Morning, Floyd,' answered Farrell.

'I want you to meet Mister Eugene MacCarthy,' said Wheeler.

'Pleased to meet you,' said Farrell as he shook hands. 'It's always a pleasure to do business with Floyd and if I can be of service to you it will be an equal pleasure.'

'Thanks,' replied MacCarthy with a smile. 'But you already have.' He saw the surprised look on the bank manager's face and hastened to add an explanation. 'Wheeler has been acting for me in this land purchasing and I must say that I am pleased with the way you have both handled things.'

'This is certainly a surprise to me,' said Farrell smiling with pleasure at the praise. He realised that MacCarthy was a man to keep in with, so he added smoothly, 'But it will be a great pleasure to work with you personally if I can be of any further service.'

'You certainly can,' replied MacCarthy.

Farrell indicated chairs to the two men and offered them both a cigar. As Mac-Carthy lit his he studied Farrell shrewdly. He judged that so long as things were going his way Farrell would play along, but if things should go wrong, or Farrell saw some other way of making extra dollars, he would not hesitate to use the information he had at his disposal. This did not worry MacCarthy, however, for he knew that if Farrell should try any double cross he had the means at his disposal to get rid of him.

When MacCarthy had his cigar drawing to his satisfaction he looked at both men in turn. 'Floyd,' he said, 'you know my ideas. Grove, I'm an ambitious man.' His eyes narrowed; a note of determination came into his voice. 'I mean to rule all this territory, and now we must turn our eyes to the ranches around here. The owners can sell out quietly or they will find there are methods of persuasion. String along with me, Farrell, and there is no telling what position you may hold in the State before we're through.'

Farrell smiled thoughtfully. 'What do you want me to do?' he asked.

'Offer a very good price for the land,' replied MacCarthy. 'It must be tempting enough to make them sell. I want things achieving peacefully if possible. And,' he added quickly, 'my name must be kept out of this. Nobody must suspect that I'm behind these offers.'

Farrell nodded. 'I've already had two inquisitive visitors,' he said, 'but they got nothing out of me.'

'Same two as I had, I expect,' said

Wheeler. 'Tom Price and Kit Sheridan.'

Farrell nodded.

'Can they cause much trouble?' asked MacCarthy.

'No,' replied Wheeler. 'Two of the smallest ranches around here. In fact, if the offer is good they might be the first to sell out.'

'Good,' said MacCarthy thoughtfully. 'Now, Farrell, I want to be seen around with you, an' you can pass me off as one of the bank officials here on a visit.'

'Very good,' said Farrell. 'I'll walk back to the hotel with you now.'

'Good idea,' replied MacCarthy.

The three men left the office and, after Floyd Wheeler left them to go to the Ace of Spades, MacCarthy and Farrell strolled along the sidewalk to the hotel.

It was a thoughtful bank manager who walked back to his office. Things were much bigger than he had expected and he knew if he played his cards right he would come out of this a very rich man, who might even possibly call the tune instead of MacCarthy.

Chapter Four

Three hundred miles to the north-east of Santa Rosa a camp fire flickered in the hills near Springfield, Colorado. Ten men warmed themselves close to the dancing flames, which lit up their grim, evil faces. Nine of them were watching and listening intently to a young man of twenty-three. His voice carried authority and he was obviously the leader of the gang, although there were men older than himself amongst them.

'We'll move into Springfield just before nine in the morning,' he said. 'The bank opens at nine o'clock and we intend to be the first customers.'

A chuckle ran through the group. 'A big withdrawal and a fast transaction,' laughed one of the men.

'Sure,' said the leader, his face unbroken by a smile. 'It will be the biggest thing thet's hit Colorado, an' if you stick to instructions nothing can go wrong, so listen carefully.'

The men knew that what he said was true. The Hart gang was notorious through three states and there was many a sheriff who would have loved to have had Bob Hart and his brother Sam behind bars. The gang respected the thoroughness with which the brothers planned raids and they knew that no detail would be overlooked.

'I've studied the town thoroughly during the past week,' said Bob, 'an' Sam has even made a couple of deposits in the bank so thet he would get a look at it. We split into two groups of five an' approach the town in opposite directions. Mosey along, easy, like, as if you're jest comin' in fer the day. Hitch your horses to the rail outside the bank, we'll need them handy fer a quick getaway. There'll be two bank clerks in the bank – the manager doesn't come in until ten. Sam will take one an' I'll take the other, with two of you to back each of us up. The other four will position themselves along the sidewalk in case of trouble.' He paused to let the instructions sink in and then delegated each man to his duty. When each man was sure of his part in the hold-up Bob Hart went on with his instructions. 'We've agreed thet this is the last time we'll operate as a gang. We've made plenty an' with this to top it off we should be set up fer the rest of our lives. If you haven't saved any then it's your own look out but Sam an' I are headin' fer Mexico. When we've pulled this off tomorrow we ride south-west fer the border of New Mexico; if we git split we meet in Clayton in four days' time.'

'The nearest we've operated to Springfield is a hundred and fifty miles,' said Sam. 'There are no wanted posters in town so we aren't likely to be recognised but I reckon we'd better burn all personal belongings thet might identify us with the raid.'

The men turned out their pockets and the fire blazed as personal items were thrown into the flames. The task completed the men rolled themselves in their blankets and tried to get some sleep.

The Hart gang were in the saddle early the next morning after breaking camp and, after splitting into two groups rode at a steady pace towards Springfield.

The town was beginning to stir as they moved at walking pace down the main street. Storemen were removing the shutters from the windows; a clerk unlocked the door of the stage office, but as yet there were few people on the sidewalks on this bright, sunny morning. Suddenly Bob Hart stiffened in the saddle and gasped with surprise. Part of the street had been torn up ready for repairs and the hitching rails outside the bank had been knocked down!

Bob cursed under his breath but kept the party to their steady walk as he drew his brother's attention to the missing hitching rails. A little fact of road repairs had upset all their careful planning and one simple essential detail now presented a problem! He was almost tempted to call a halt to the whole project but as they passed the bank the doors swung open; it was nine o'clock! He turned into the road beside the bank and then into the alley which ran behind the building. Half a block further down there was a rail where they dismounted and tied their horses. The second party, who had noted Bob's alteration of plan, as they rode down the main street, joined them. The horses needed for a quick get-away were not so handy but with any luck they could still succeed.

Each man pulled his rifle from the saddle boot and eased his Colt in its holster. They were so intent on getting to the bank that they failed to notice a man who turned into the alley one block away. Immediately he saw the armed men he was suspicious and turned back quickly out of sight. Peering carefully round the corner he took another look at the men and, in spite of the disguise of false beards and moustaches, he thought he recognised some members of the Hart gang. He ran quickly back to Main Street which he crossed at a brisk walk without drawing undue attention to himself. He saw the outlaws turn into the main street as he reached the hardware store opposite the bank. He opened the door and stepped inside.

''Mornin' Jeb,' greeted the store-keeper. 'What's matter with you? Look as if you've seen a ghost.'

'Look, Dave,' said Jeb pointing through the window at the men who were disappearing into the bank. 'I reckon thet's the Hart gang! I spent a couple of years up north an' I think I recognised Sam Hart.'

The note of urgency in Jeb's voice made Dave realise how serious he was. He did not hesitate for a moment and the two citizens of Springfield set in motion events which were to have repercussions three hundred miles away in Santa Rosa.

'We'll hev a few precious moments before they git any money,' said Dave. 'Git outside an' warn anyone you can, if they aren't carryin' a gun send them in here an' I'll hand out some rifles.'

Jeb hurried from the store but without a

haste which would arouse the suspicions of the outlaws guarding the entrance to the bank. Inconspicuously, citizens of Springfield prepared a reception for the outlaws.

As they entered the bank the robbers drew their Colts and two startled clerks found themselves looking at threatening guns. They threw up their hands quickly and backed away from the counter.

'Open the safe, quick,' snapped Bob.

'I can't,' answered the terrified clerk.

'Don't lie,' snarled Sam, 'I've seen you do it. Get it open, pronto.' He clicked back the hammer of his Colt ominously.

The frightened man, fumbling in his pocket for the key, turned to the safe. Bob, followed by two outlaws with a sack, hurried round the counter. He shoved the clerk roughly.

'Hurry!' he snarled.

The clerk drew the key from his pocket but in his haste dropped it. He stooped to pick it up and then, shaking with terror, fumbled as he put it into the lock. Unknown to him, this unintentional attempt to delay the robber by the clerk was giving the people of Springfield those few moments they needed.

The safe swung open and, as Bob kept the clerk covered, the two outlaws stepped forward and, ignoring the silver as being too heavy, scooped the notes out of the safe into the sack.

'Must be over forty thousand here,' grinned one of the men.

'All right, quit the talking,' snapped Bob impatiently. 'Give the sack to Sam.' The man threw the sack on to the counter where Sam Hart grabbed it and turned for the door. 'Wait a moment, Sam,' called Bob. 'We'll all leave together.' He turned to the two outlaws. 'Deal with them,' he instructed nodding to the clerks. The two men dealt swiftly with the clerks leaving them unconscious on the floor.

Hurrying to the door the outlaws stepped outside and their appearance was the signal for a withering fusillade of bullets from the townsfolk. The two outlaws, who left the bank in front of the Hart brothers, pitched on to the wooden boards before they knew what was happening. Momentarily the brothers stopped, staring at each other, amazed by this unexpected reception. The shots had all been directed at the bank door and this allowed the four outlaws on the sidewalk to send lead flying in defence of the Harts. Using the covering fire Bob and Sam leaped through the doorway, dashed for the side road followed by the two other men who had been in the bank. The other four men covered their companions as they too retreated.

Bullets flew around the robbers as they reached the side road. One man halted in his tracks, staggered for a few yards and then pitched head first into the dust as a third bullet crashed into his back. Bob Hart and two of his men were sprinting hard down the street followed by Sam who clung desperately to the sack. They were covered by the other three men who kept up a steady fire as they retreated. The townspeople of Springfield poured lead after the fleeing men wounding two of them in the arms. Bob reached the safety of the alley and raced for the horses. He unhitched both his own and his brother's and turned towards the side road. Two of the outlaws were already in the saddle and racing away at a fast gallop. The two wounded men ran round the corner and dashed for their mounts. Bob held the horses impatiently. Where was Sam? Suddenly he appeared staggering backwards, still clutching the sack and blazing away with his Colt. 'Hang on!' Bob yelled, urging the horses forward. Sam pitched on to his knees, a look of agony on his face. The remaining outlaw jumped to

Sam's side but as he got his arm round him he staggered backwards under the impact of a bullet in his shoulder. He twisted and dived for cover. Bob, racing towards his brother, pulled hard on the reins as he neared the corner. He leaped from the saddle before the horse stopped and threw the reins to the wounded man who had staggered to his feet. The man grasped the reins eagerly with his sound hand and held the horses firmly. The firing had ceased and Bob heard men yelling on Main Street as they ran from the stores and offices. He waited momentarily, staring at his brother lying face downwards in the street, a sack still firmly gripped in his hand, then he leaped from his cover. Crouching, his face dark with hatred for this town, he blazed away at the men running up the street. They dived for cover and Bob seized the respite to grasp his brother in his powerful arms. His eyes filled with horror when he saw the four bullet holes in Sam's back and the blood which oozed to stain the dust of Springfield. Sam groaned as Bob turned him over.

'I'm done,' gasped Sam. 'Get out, Bob.'

'Not without you,' yelled Bob as he lifted Sam and turned for cover.

A bullet whipped past his head and

another clipped the dust at his feet.

'It's no … use,' groaned Sam. 'Leave me… I … can't go…' his voice trailed away. The sack fell from his grasp and lay in the street.

Bullets whistled close to Bob as he staggered to the horses behind the cover of the buildings. He looked at his brother, he hung limp, his head thrown back, his eyes staring unseeing. Bob laid him down and stood for a moment gazing at the man with whom he had shared all his life.

'Come on!' yelled a voice in his ear.

The wounded outlaw shoved the reins into Bob's hand and pulled himself up into the saddle of Sam's horse. He turned the animal round and kicked it furiously into an earth pounding gallop.

Startled back to reality Bob was suddenly galvanised into action when he heard the yells and pound of running feet. He glanced at the sack lying in the dust but knew it would be suicide to attempt to get it. He swung quickly into the saddle, pulled his horse round sharply and sent it away at a fast gallop.

Four outlaws were already clearing the town as the fifth man with Bob close on his heels swung out of the alley into the main street three blocks away from the bank.

Confusion reigned behind them but their appearance on Main Street brought a quick but useless fusillade of shots. Bob and the wounded man thundered out of Springfield following a dust cloud which was rising ahead of them.

In the confusion in Springfield it was some minutes before the sheriff was able to form a posse and that time was valuable to the outlaws. They had covered about four miles at a dead run when Bob realised that the man beside him was swaying in the saddle. He eased the pace and turned his attention to the wounded man. His arm hung limp by his side and blood poured from a shattered wrist and an ugly hole in his shoulder. The man's face was creased in pain as he swayed precariously in the saddle. It took all the energy he could muster to remain upright on his horse. Bob moved closer to his companion and leaning forward in the saddle grasped the reins to ease both animals to a halt.

'I'd better hev a look at the wounds, Pete,' he said.

Pete's face was drained of colour. He stared dimly at Bob. 'Git goin'...' he gulped. 'I'm done ... fer ... better leave me here... I...' his voice trailed away and, before Bob could grab hold of him, he slipped sideways

63

in the saddle to fall heavily to the ground and into unconsciousness.

Bob swung off his horse quickly and dropped on one knee beside the outlaw. Pete was breathing faintly and, after getting his canteen of water, Bob bathed his wounds and bound them up with his neckerchief. He worked quickly and methodically and it was only when he had done what he could that he turned his attention to their pursuers. The tell-tale dust cloud was still some considerable distance away and Bob knew that the people from Springfield could not possibly see them at that distance.

Looking in the other direction he saw that the dust raised by the four escaping outlaws was rapidly disappearing towards the horizon. There was no chance of attracting their attention for help and with a wounded man there was no hope of out-running their pursuers. He looked round sharply, seeking some cover. The ground to the left sloped away and dropped into an arroyo, the sides of which were strewn with rocks and shrubs. Bob realised that his only chance was to reach that cover quickly and hope that the dust cloud of the four men ahead would act as a decoy to the men from Springfield.

As he struggled to lift Pete the man

regained some measure of consciousness.

'Leave me,' he gasped.

Bob shook his head. 'No!' he snapped. 'There's a chance if we git down there,' he added nodding towards the arroyo.

Pete grasped the saddle with his sound hand and took some of his weight as Bob lifted him into the saddle. The effort drained his remaining strength and he slumped forward in the saddle. Bob pushed Pete's feet into the stirrups and gathering the reins of both horses he led them off the trail and picked his way down the slope to the arroyo. He led the horses quickly over the rocky ground until he found suitable cover out of sight of the trail. He tied the horses securely, helped Pete from the saddle and laid him gently on the ground. Drawing his Colt he positioned himself so that he could watch the trail.

As the pound of hooves grew louder Bob tensed himself, prepared to sell his life dearly and revenge his brother's death. So intent were the riders on following the tell-tale cloud of dust that they failed to notice any signs of Bob Hart's deviation from the trail.

As the hoof-beats faded into the distance Bob breathed a sigh of relief and relaxed. The tension of immediate pursuit had gone but he realised that they would have to move carefully as they headed south for the pre-arranged meeting place at Clayton.

Bob hurried back to Pete. 'We've lost them,' he said trying to sound cheerful as he sat down beside the wounded man.

Pete smiled wanly.

'How you feelin'?' asked Bob.

Pete shook his head. 'I'll never make Clayton,' he whispered hoarsely.

'Course you will,' replied Bob. 'We'll rest up a while an' then head south slowly, takin' our time, an' gettin' you well.'

'You'd be better goin' alone,' replied Pete. 'I'll slow you down an' make it more dangerous fer you.'

'I'll not leave you,' replied Bob firmly and stopped Pete as he started to protest again.

Pete knew it was useless to argue; Bob Hart might be a notorious outlaw, but he had a strong sense of loyalty to his own men.

'What went wrong today?' asked Pete.

'Jest wasn't our day,' replied Bob. 'I never reckoned on the hitchin' rail being down an' I figure someone must hev recognised us. We've never operated as far south before so it must hev been someone from the north – jest our luck.'

After resting for a couple of hours Bob decided to push on, but, as he helped Pete to his feet, the wound started to bleed freely again and Pete's fit of coughing was accompanied by the spitting of blood.

'Guess we can't go yet,' observed Bob, easing Pete back to the ground. 'Seems as if one of those bullets in your shoulder did more damage than I thought.'

Pete nodded weakly. For two days his condition grew worse, for two days Bob stayed by his side in spite of Pete's pleadings to go. Bob even suggested giving themselves up so that a doctor could attend to Pete, but Pete dissuaded him telling him that it would be foolish to keep a man alive in order to put a noose round his neck. It was late on the second day when Pete died and Bob buried him under some trees close to the arroyo. Once Bob was on the move again he headed southwards at a good pace, avoiding all contact with other human beings.

Three days later Bob Hart rode slowly up the deserted street of the ghost town of Clayton. His keen eyes searched for some sign of life but the only sound which greeted him was the sighing of the soft wind as it played around the deserted, broken buildings. His horse barely stirred the dust as it walked slowly down the centre of the street. Suddenly the broken batwings of what had once been the saloon were flung open and six men with Colts in hand appeared. Bob stiffened pulling his horse to a halt. His eyes narrowed when he saw the star pinned to the brown shirt of one of the men as they stepped into the roadway and ranged themselves across the outlaw's path. Bob's brain raced. These were the men he had seen as he hid in the arroyo. How had they found the meeting place? Had they captured the rest of the gang and made someone talk?

His thoughts were interrupted by the sheriff. 'Bob Hart, I'm arrestin' you for murder.' A smile split the lawman's face. 'It will give the people of Springfield a lot of pleasure to see you swingin' from a rope.'

Bob remained calm. 'How did you know where to find me?' he asked.

'Wal, I played a hunch,' replied the sheriff only too pleased to boast of how he caught the notorious Bob Hart. 'I knew you had split up an' therefore must hev a pre-arranged meeting place. I followed some of you fer a long way south an' reckoned you were headin' fer the border of New Mexico. I figured a ghost town was a likely rendez-vous and Clayton was close to the border.'

He grinned triumphantly. 'Wal, it seems I was right. Now all we hev to do is to wait for the rest of your gang.'

Bob's brain pounded. He was the first to be caught; maybe there would still be a chance to escape!

Suddenly the smile vanished from the sheriff's face. His eyes narrowed. 'Git down off thet horse,' he snapped, moving forward to grasp Bob.

Before his hand closed round the outlaw's arm a rifle cracked and a surprised look of disbelief crossed the sheriff's face as he pitched forward into the dust beside Bob's horse. Guns roared and bullets flew across the street. As Bob flung himself from the saddle he saw three of the men stagger and fall before they realised what was happening. He hit the ground and rolled over, his hand reaching for his Colt. One of the remaining men loosed off a shot which spurted the dust close to the outlaw but, before he could fire again, a bullet from Bob's Colt spun him backwards to the ground. Shocked by the swiftness of the slaughter the remaining man stood rooted to the spot and before his rifle reached his shoulder he was cut down by a bullet from an unseen assailant.

When he saw him hit the dust Bob lay still,

his gun trained on the bodies but he saw no movement. The sound of running feet pounded behind him and he twisted over to face his rescuers. He gasped with surprise when he saw four of his gang running towards him. A grin split his face as he pushed himself to his feet, holstered his gun and hurried to meet the four men.

They grasped his hands and slapped him on the back.

'Glad to see you, boss!'

'How did you make out?'

'What happened to the others?'

'Where's Sam?'

Bob's grin disappeared at the mention of his brother's name. Seeing the look which came across his face the four men quietened and stared almost disbelievingly at their leader.

'Not dead?' whispered one.

Bob nodded grimly. 'I'm the only other one thet's left. Sam was cut down in the side street,' he said. He turned and stared hatefully at the bodies which littered the street. 'I reckon we've hed our revenge.' He paused a moment then turned to his companions. 'Was I mighty glad to see you!' he went on, a brighter tone in his voice. 'But what happened, Red? They said you weren't here.'

70

'We gave them the slip an' came on here,' explained Red, 'but they must hev played a hunch comin' here. Fortunately, Jake an' Russ spotted them coming an' we managed to slip out of town an' hide in those low hills a quarter of a mile away. We watched the posse search the town thoroughly an', figurin' they wouldn't do it again, we left the horses out there an' sneaked back into town when it was dark. We had to be here when you arrived.'

'I'm mighty glad you were,' grinned Bob. 'Smart work, boys. Russ, Wade, you were wounded, how are you?'

'Only flesh wounds,' replied Wade. 'We're all right.'

'What do we do now?' asked Red.

'Wal, I reckon we'd better git out of here fast. The whole State will be on the look out fer us when they find this,' said Bob, nodding in the direction of the dead men. 'The sooner we're over the border into New Mexico the better. After this there'll be a bigger price on our heads, an' thet'll attract the bounty hunters. I figure we'd better hole up somewhere fer awhile. Russ, you used to know New Mexico, any ideas?'

Russ looked thoughtful as they headed out of Clayton to collect the horses. 'Yeah,' he

71

drawled, 'I think I know the place. Somewhere between the Canadian and Pecos Rivers, jest north of Santa Rosa. It's rugged country an' we could hide out in one of the canyons.'

'Good,' answered Bob. 'We'll lie up there fer awhile an' then head fer Mexico One more job in some place like Langtry close to the border an' we'll be set fer the rest of our lives.'

Chapter Five

As Kit Sheridan sat down for his breakfast his wife, Mabel, came in with an envelope in her hand.

'I've just found this,' she said, handing the envelope to her husband. 'It must have been pushed under the door during the night.'

Sheridan picked up a knife and slit open the envelope. He pulled out a sheet of paper, unfolded it and read its contents quickly.

'Well, I'll be blowed,' he gasped.

'What is it, Kit?' asked his wife who was pouring the coffee.

Sheridan stared at the paper in his hand.

'I'm offered twenty thousand dollars fer the ranch!' His voice filled with awe was scarcely above a whisper.

'What!' gasped Mrs Sheridan. Her tone was one of disbelief. 'It can't be right.' She reached for the letter. 'Here, let me see,' she said.

Kit handed her the letter. She read through it quickly, sank slowly into a chair beside the table and stared at her husband. It was a moment before either of them spoke.

'What are you going to do?' she asked.

Sheridan shook his head slowly. 'I don't know,' he whispered, 'but it's an awful lot of money fer the Circle J.'

Mrs Sheridan glanced at the letter. 'This is signed by Grove Farrell on behalf of an unknown client,' she said, 'I wonder who it is.'

Kit shook his head thoughtfully. 'I don't know,' he muttered. 'An' thet's the part I don't like. I'd rather know who I was dealin' with.'

'Then don't sell,' replied his wife. 'I'm not particular to leave here; we've got nicely settled and things are going well. If we move we'll have to start all over again and I must say I wouldn't relish that.'

Kit leaned forward and patted his wife's hand. 'I know how you feel, Mabel, an' I must say I'd be content to stay here; but that isn't the complete picture.'

'What do you mean?' asked Mabel curiously.

'Wal, with thet amount of money we could buy a place with half of it and the other half would go a long way to makin' us comfortably off for the rest of our lives,' explained her husband.

'But I thought an association had been formed to resist the efforts of this unknown buyer,' said Mrs Sheridan.

'Thet's true,' replied Kit, 'but this is such a good price. If the other ranchers hev had similar offers an' they sell out then we could be left in a very awkward position dominated by a big spread. Things could get so tough thet we'd hev to sell an' of course we wouldn't git such a good offer then.'

'Don't you see,' replied his wife urgently, 'that this offer has probably been made to cause unrest amongst you. Your strength lies in unity; if one weakens then you can all sell out. The sooner you contact the others the better.'

Kit nodded, 'You're right, Mabel,' he said, 'I'll go to see Tom right away an' hev my breakfast when I get back.' He pushed himself away from the table but, before he had

74

time to reach the door, the pound of hooves sent them both hurrying outside.

Tom Price pulled his horse to a halt in front of the Sheridans.

'Look what I've got this morning,' Tom panted as he stepped on to the verandah and handed a letter to Kit. Kit gave it a quick glance.

'Same as I've got,' he said handing it back to Price.

'What!' gasped Tom. 'Same price?' Kit nodded. 'But where's all the money comin' from?' said Tom. 'It's fantastic; someone means to hev all the land around here. It's a temptin' offer. What are you goin' to do, Kit?'

'Wal, I'm married,' replied Sheridan. 'In spite of the tempting offer we don't feel as if we want to move again.'

'But the money...' started Price.

'It's a lot,' cut in Sheridan. He looked hard at his friend. 'I thought we formed an association to fight this sort of land grabbing.'

'I know,' replied Price, 'but we never expected an offer like this.'

'But if one sells it weakens the position of those that are left,' pointed out Kit.

Price nodded and looked thoughtful. 'It sure is a lot of money fer the Running W,' he whispered half to himself. Suddenly he turned to Kit, excitement showing in his voice. 'It's a glorious chance to rid ourselves of the debt we owe on the two spreads.'

Kit looked serious. 'Yes, I know,' he agreed, 'but the way things have been goin' we'll be rid of that in two years, an' then we'll hev a steady income, which, over the years, will mount up, and above all we'll be settled. Another thing, Tom, we did agree to stay united throughout this business, no matter what happened.'

'Shore we did,' replied Tom, 'but an offer like this is different. I'll tell you what, we won't decide anything until we see what the others say.'

'All right,' agreed Kit and the two men left the house. They heard similar stories from all the ranchers who had formed the association and it was only after a long discussion in which Mark Stevens played a prominent part that they decided to turn the offer down and to stick together.

'Wish I knew who was makin' these offers,' said Kit Sheridan.

'Can't be one man,' said Abe.

'I'll bet it's like I said,' said Price. 'Frank McCoy's the richest rancher around here and if he teamed up with Floyd Wheeler, who must be makin' a packet out of the Ace

76

of Spades, they could get the backin' of the bank an' they'd be in a position to make these offers.'

'Still harping on those lines,' snapped Mark. 'Frank's all right; let's go and see him; if he's had an offer then thet blows your ideas sky high.'

'Not necessarily so,' replied Price. 'He could hev sent an offer to himself as a blind.'

Mark glared angrily at Price. 'Won't anythin' ever convince you?' he shouted. 'C'm on let's go and see Frank.'

The ranchers hurried to their horses, and Mark, sullen in his anger, kept the men to a fast pace. Frank McCoy was busy breaking in some horses when he heard the riders approaching. Handing over to one of his ranch-hands he walked over to the corral fence, climbed the rails and sat astride them until the horsemen drew rein.

'You fellahs doin' a lot of ridin' together lately,' grinned Frank, 'What brings you this time?'

'Get any letters this mornin'?' snapped Price before Mark could speak.

'Sure, I got a temptin' offer fer the Lazy A,' answered Frank, guessing that this was what Price wanted to know. 'I reckon you fellahs must hev had offers too.'

Mark turned to Price; 'There you are,' he said, 'this proves…'

'Nothin',' cut in Price. 'How did he know we got letters if he didn't send them?'

Frank grinned. 'It wasn't hard to guess seein' you all ride here together at this time of the mornin'.'

'We only hev his word; we hevn't seen the letter,' said Price.

'It's in the house there,' snapped Frank irritably. 'You can go an' see it.'

Price started to turn his horse but was halted by Abe Carson. 'Thet won't be necessary, Frank,' he said quietly. 'We believe you.' He turned to Price. 'It wouldn't prove anythin' if you saw it, Tom.'

Price glared thoughtfully. 'Guess you're right.'

'Look here, McCoy,' said Sheridan, 'we've all got these letters an' we've all decided to turn the offer down.'

'Glad to hear it,' said Frank. 'So have I.'

'Then surely now is the time for an association to really work,' went on Sheridan.

'Don't think so,' replied Frank. 'Turn the offer down an' thet's that.'

'Don't you believe it,' shouted Price. 'A man thet makes all these offers wants the land badly an' he isn't jest goin' to take no

78

fer an answer.'

'I think Price is right,' put in Wes Briton. 'We must remain strongly united.'

Frank shook his head. 'It'll lead to trouble.'

Price spat angrily with disgust. He pulled his horse hard round. 'I'm goin' to see Grove Farrell,' he yelled. 'Anybody comin'?'

The other six riders turned their horses and kicked them forward. Mark shot a glance at Frank who grinned back at him and watched his friend ride after the other ranchers.

Eugene MacCarthy was in Floyd Wheeler's office when he heard the thunder of hooves in the main street. Both men glanced at each other and crossed to the window to see the seven ranchers pull their horses to a stop in front of the bank.

'Well, there they go,' grinned Wheeler, 'all goin' in together. The territory will soon be yours.'

MacCarthy turned from the window as the last man entered the bank. 'I'm not so sure,' he said thoughtfully. 'Looks as if they're actin' together an' thet can only spell resistance.'

'There's one missing,' said Wheeler quietly.

'Who's that?' asked MacCarthy.

'McCoy,' answered Floyd.

'The strongest of them all,' whispered MacCarthy between tight lips, annoyance showing on his face. 'If only it had been one of the weaker ones.'

'Maybe they'll all sell out,' pointed out Wheeler. 'They were mighty temptin' offers you put out. I don't know where you're gettin' all the cash from.'

'There are ways and means,' said MacCarthy, 'and when I hev all the territory I'll make it back and more.' A look of ambitious greed had crept into his eyes as visions of a state ruled by Eugene MacCarthy were conjured up. 'And you'll be in it with me, Floyd,' he went on. 'We'll run things thet will...'

'They're comin' out!' interrupted Wheeler, who had been watching the bank all the time. MacCarthy was by his side in a flash and after seeing the ranchers mount their horses and ride away he turned from the window.

'C'm on,' he said. 'We'll see what's happened.'

The two men were soon at the bank and without waiting to be announced they hurried into Farrell's office. The bank manager looked startled at the suddenness of the interruption.

'Well?' snapped MacCarthy.

Farrell shook his head slowly. 'Not one of them would sell. I told them they weren't likely to get another offer as good but it was no use.'

MacCarthy, disappointment showing on his face, smacked his right fist into the palm of his left hand. 'Then we'll fight them!' he hissed venomously.

'They gave me a message to pass on to whoever was making the offer,' said Farrell.

'Well, what was it?' snapped MacCarthy.

'They said that they were united and if any trouble started they'd be ready to meet force with force,' explained Farrell. 'I assured them my client was not that kind of man.'

'Isn't he?' snapped MacCarthy. 'I'll make every one of them wish he'd accepted my offer. Before I'm through they'll come begging to be bought out!' Both Farrell and Wheeler were surprised at the venomous, hateful tone of MacCarthy's voice. 'Now to get down to some details,' he went on, his tone changing to one of purposeful determination. He sat down opposite the bank manager. 'First, I want some information from you,' he said. 'Give me the details of the financial positions of all the ranchers.'

Farrell looked surprised at the request.

'But Mister MacCarthy I daren't...'

'Don't play the innocent with me, Farrell,' snarled MacCarthy. 'This game is going to be played dirty now, so I pull all the stops out. Thet information, Farrell, or someone will get to know about your illegal dealing to git rich quick before you came to Santa Rosa.'

Farrell's eyes widened with surprise.

'Oh, yes, we know all about it,' grinned MacCarthy. 'So you'd be wise not to get on the wrong side of me.'

Farrell squirmed in his chair, hating the man in front of him. He realised he was powerless to refuse. He was a man who revelled in the power he held over men as their bank manager, able to refuse loans if he wished or loan only so much that a man's ambitions were kept irritatingly just out of his reach. But now he felt the power of another man, and he hated MacCarthy for wielding it.

'Come on,' snapped MacCarthy.

Farrell pushed himself reluctantly from his desk and crossed to a safe in the wall from which he extracted a big ledger. After telling the clerks at the counter that he did not wish to be disturbed he returned to his desk and the three men studied the private accounts of all the ranchers.

After half an hour's careful study Mac-Carthy seemed satisfied. 'Well,' he said, 'That puts me in the picture nicely. Thanks, Farrell.' He grinned at the bank manager. 'Don't take it too hard. You're on the right side.' He rose from his chair. 'Come on, Floyd, we have things to plan.'

There was hate in his eyes as Grove Farrell stared at the door which shut behind the two men. 'Blackmail, is it?' he hissed. 'Two can play at that game Mister MacCarthy an' before I'm through may be I'll be calling the tune.'

'Farrell didn't like our information,' observed MacCarthy as the two men strolled along the sidewalk. 'He could be dangerous, Floyd, so put Butch Lant on to watch him. You can also draw up a list of men who ride hard an' fight hard; we're goin' to need them.'

Suddenly he stopped, grasping Wheeler's arm to halt him. MacCarthy stared at a cowboy who was pulling his horse to a halt in front of the General Store about fifty yards along the street. The man, who kept his head bowed as if wanting to avoid notice, swung from the saddle, and stepped quickly across the sidewalk into the store.

MacCarthy, who had studied him intently, hurried forward and peered cautiously through the window of the shop.

'What's the matter?' whispered Wheeler pretending to examine the goods in the window.

'I think I recognise that man,' replied MacCarthy but offered no more information.

The two men watched as the man bought provisions. 'From what that hombre's buying I reckon he has some friends hereabouts; wouldn't you say so, Floyd?' said Mac-Carthy.

'It figures,' replied Wheeler. 'But who is he?'

The man had finished buying and the storekeeper was reckoning up the bill. Mac-Carthy gripped Wheeler's arm and turned away from the window. They strolled a few yards along the sidewalk and leaned on the rail.

'Ever heard of the Hart gang?' asked MacCarthy keeping his voice low.

'Yeah,' replied Wheeler, 'but they operate in northern Colorado so what's this got to do with thet hombre?'

'Thet's where I've seen the gang and the "Wanted" posters,' said MacCarthy. 'I've a good memory for faces an' I reckon he's one of them.'

'But they've never operated as far south as this?' pointed out Wheeler.

'They attempted to rob the bank in Springfield in southern Colorado a few days ago but the raid was a failure; the gang got shot up rather badly. It could be thet the remnants hev moved south an' are holed-up somewhere near here,' explained Mac-Carthy.

'Could be,' agreed Wheeler.

MacCarthy rubbed his chin thoughtfully. 'If they are about,' he said, 'they could be just the men we need.'

Wheeler grinned as he realised the significance of MacCarthy's words. 'I've got to hand it to you, Eugene, you are quick to seize chances,' he said.

'Thet's why I've got where I am today,' replied MacCarthy, 'and thet's why I'm going to boss this whole state.' Suddenly he gripped Wheeler's arm. The man had emerged from the store. 'Get me a horse quick,' whispered MacCarthy.

Wheeler crossed the road quickly un-hitched his horse from the rail outside the saloon and walked back towards MacCarthy.

By the time MacCarthy took the reins the man had loaded his horse and was riding along the street.

'Keep your eye on any developments until I get back,' instructed MacCarthy, and with a curt nod to Wheeler he swung into the saddle and sent his horse along Main Street.

The stranger kept his mount to a walking pace until he was out of the town and then put the animal into a steady trot. Mac-Carthy matched the pace and was not surprised when after about three miles, the man left the north road and cut into the hills. The route took them through a wide valley of lush grass with the hills on either side rising to a backcloth of huge snow-capped mountains. Ahead lay huge peaks and MacCarthy realised from his study of maps of the area that they were travelling through land recently purchased by Frank McCoy in his Black Water Canyon deal and that the Canyon itself lay ahead.

As they moved further along the valley, climbing all the time, the grass became sparser and eventually gave way to a bare, rocky terrain. The hills steepened and closed in on either side until the two riders were moving through a narrow canyon along which flowed a deep stream, he had noticed in the valley, fed by the snows of the magnificent peaks ahead. Recognising the potentialities of the valley and the lower reaches of the canyon, coupled with a marvellous supply of water, MacCarthy was annoyed that he had been beaten to its purchase by McCoy.

As the canyon narrowed and twisted MacCarthy closed the distance between himself and the rider ahead. He was thankful that he had done so, for as he cautiously rounded a bend, he was just in time to see the man turn into a narrow cleft in the cliff-like face of the canyon. The cleft ran back into the wall of rock and after about a hundred yards the floor of the cleft began to rise sharply. MacCarthy proceeded with utmost caution leading his horse along the path which led on to a shelf above Black Water Canyon. Ten yards further on the path left the shelf and spilled over the cliff top into a hollow. MacCarthy found himself amongst an upheaval of rocks and boulders beyond which the ground sloped into the bowl-shaped hollow in the centre of which MacCarthy could see a camp occupied by four men.

He surveyed the scene for a few moments and was about to move forward when a harsh voice broke the silence behind him.

'Hold it!'

MacCarthy froze in his tracks. He heard footsteps scraping the rocks behind him as the man picked his way carefully towards him. He felt the hard muzzle of a gun pressed into the small of his back.

'Leave the horse; raise your hands an' move forward, easy like,' ordered his captor.

MacCarthy did as he was told and a few moments later he saw the men in the camp look in their direction and then scramble to their feet to face them. One man stepped forward.

'Russ, I told you to be careful you weren't followed,' he snapped angrily.

'Sorry, boss,' answered Russ. 'I didn't know there was someone on my tail until I was in the cleft leading out of the Canyon.'

The first man glared at MacCarthy. 'Who are you?' he rapped.

'Eugene MacCarthy,' came the reply.

'Never heard of you.'

MacCarthy smiled. 'Maybe not but I know you. You're Bob Hart an' I figure this is all thet's left of your gang after the Springfield hold up.'

Hart's eyes narrowed. He was both angry and annoyed that they had been discovered in a hide-out which he had thought perfect.

'Seems you know more than is good for you,' he snarled.

'My knowledge can benefit you,' replied

MacCarthy quietly.

Hart looked curiously at the man in front of him. He was puzzled. In spite of the fact he was at the mercy of the gang MacCarthy was calm, a flicker of a supercilious smile on his lips, it was as if he held the trump card.

'What do you mean?' asked Hart cautiously. 'Why did you follow Russ?'

'I've seen the "Wanted" posters in north Colorado; as a matter of fact I was in Greeley when you got away with thirty thousand dollars; I recognised Russ when he was in town,' explained MacCarthy.

'Why didn't you hand him over to the law?' asked Hart curiously.

'I wanted to find out where you were,' explained MacCarthy.

'Yeah, so you could hand us *all* over to the sheriff,' snarled Russ. 'I'd better put a bullet in him, boss.'

'Hold it,' ordered Hart. 'I'm curious. What's on your mind, MacCarthy?'

MacCarthy grinned and looked past Hart at the fire. 'I see you hev some coffee ready,' he said. 'I think we might as well hev a cup whilst we talk things over.'

Hart hesitated a moment, amazed at the coolness of this man.

'All right,' he agreed. 'But whatever you

hev to tell us hed better be good or you won't leave here alive.'

The men moved round the fire, seated themselves on the ground and watched MacCarthy as he sipped the coffee.

'Wal?' snapped Hart, impatient at the delay.

MacCarthy smiled. 'All in good time, I'm enjoying this coffee.' When he had finished his drink and lit a cheroot MacCarthy stood up. 'I need a bunch of men like you to work for me,' he said, pacing slowly up and down. 'I've got big plans to run this whole territory. I've been purchasing a lot of land around Santa Rosa, and now I want to take over that which is owned by certain ranchers.'

'Why don't you buy it from them?' asked Hart.

'I've already made them some very good offers and they've all turned them down,' answered MacCarthy. 'Now they need a little persuasion,' he added with a grin, 'and I want a bunch of hard hitting, hard riding men. When I saw Russ in town I figured you were about and I reckoned you'd be interested.'

'Yeah, sure,' said Bob Hart, 'but we're on the run, headin' fer Mexico.'

'You're safe enough here, besides, when I rule the territory I'll be the law and if you're working for me you'll be working for the law.'

The outlaws grinned. 'Git this,' laughed Jake, 'the Hart gang – lawmen.'

'Quiet,' snapped Bob. 'This is serious.' He paused thoughtfully. 'If we ride fer you, MacCarthy, then we can stop runnin'!'

'Yes,' agreed MacCarthy. 'And make yourself a nice pile of cash, in complete safety.'

'This is interesting,' said Bob. 'Tell us more about it.'

MacCarthy put the outlaws in the picture. 'The first thing to do is to get these ranchers out,' he went on, 'then I'll have all the land round Santa Rosa and thet means we can control the town. With Floyd Wheeler running the Ace of Spades for me I already have a foothold and a useful source of income. It's your first job to see these ranchers toe the line.'

'It seems a good proposition to me,' said the outlaw leader looking at his men. They gave their approval and Bob Hart held out his hand to MacCarthy who took it in a firm grip. 'Do we work in the open?' asked Bob.

'Not yet,' replied MacCarthy. 'Nobody can connect me with anything and I don't want them to for a while. You can work from here. Start on the small ranchers and work through to the bigger men, Stevens and McCoy.' MacCarthy went on to explain the set up of the ranchers. 'Just one other thing,' he concluded. 'If anyone is moving through these mountains keep tag on them but leave them alone unless absolutely necessary, and watch out for this McCoy, he's tough from all I hear and you're on his land.'

Chapter Six

Leaving their horses secured in a clump of trees on the hillside behind the Circle J ranch-house, Bob Hart and his gang moved cautiously forward until they were in a position from which they overlooked the house. The first signs of night were moving in the sky when they saw Kit Sheridan and his two hired hands ride in, tired after a long day in the saddle. They stabled their horses and, eager for the evening meal, hurried to the house.

For the past three days the Hart gang had studied the layout of the Circle J and Running W ranches as well as exploring Black Water Canyon and its neighbouring canyons, and now the study was to be put to use. Ten minutes later Bob gave the signal and he, together with Jake, Red and Russ, slipped quickly down the gently sloping hillside towards the ranch-house. Wade waited until he saw them nearing the bottom before hurrying back to the trees to return to the edge of the hill with the horses.

Bob Hart positioned himself beside some fencing so that he had both the front and back doors in view. He drew his Colt and signalled to his men to go into action. Jake and Red slipped quickly towards two corrals in which there were some of Sheridan's best cattle. Russ moved swiftly to the back of the house where he lit some prepared torches and threw them on to the roof. As the flames took hold of the timbers Russ sprinted to the stables where he quickly released the horses and set fire to the piles of hay. When he left the stable and ran towards the hillside he saw that Jake and Red had already opened the coral gates and were sprinting towards Wade who was riding down the hillside with the horses.

The attack had been so swift that when Sheridan and his men raced from the house confusion reigned; flames leaped from the house and stable, horses pounded away from the fire and cattle poured from the corrals. Bob Hart raised his gun; his first two shots dropped the hired hands but the third shot was that fraction of a second too late. Kit Sheridan was diving for cover when the bullet smashed into his shoulder flinging him over near the house which was now blazing furiously. Mrs Sheridan, her eyes wide with fear, grabbed at her husband to drag him to safety.

Bob Hart leaped to his feet and raced towards Wade who flung the reins to the men as they leaped into the saddle. They pulled the animals round sending them forward after the earth-pounding steers. The cattle were soon under control and the outlaws manoeuvred them towards the mountains. When he was satisfied that everything was under control Hart pulled his horse to a halt and turned to see that the house and stable were a mass of roaring flames which lit up the darkening sky. With a satisfied grin Bob Hart sent his horse forward intent on seeing the cattle to the hiding place which they had discovered the previous day.

A mile from Black Water Canyon the outlaws turned the cattle into a huge cleft which ran back into the mountains parallel to the Canyon. Bob Hart rode ahead and took up a position near a cut in the rock face which appeared to lead only into a wall of rock but which turned and led into a small secluded, grassy valley bounded on all sides by precipitous cliffs.

Hart urged the first steers through the cutting and by steady patient work they got the hundred head of cattle into the valley before it was too dark. After rolling two boulders across the mouth of the cutting the outlaws made their way to the opposite end of the valley where they entered a cleft only wide enough for a horse. After blocking this entrance so no cattle could stray they traversed the narrow cutting which led into Black Water Canyon. Hart led the way from the canyon to their hideout and five tired men were soon enjoying a meal.

'Nice work,' congratulated Bob. 'Don't be long before you get some sleep, we ride early in the morning.'

Tom Price was enjoying a meal when he glanced out of the window and was startled to see a glow in the sky.

'Fire!' he gasped. 'Near Kit's!' He leaped to his feet, grabbed his Stetson and ran from the house. He raced to the stable, saddled his horse and was soon galloping towards the Circle J. As he neared the ranch he was shocked to see the buildings a mass of leaping, devouring flames. Racing forward he saw Kit's two hired hands lying in crumpled heaps near the house and a short distance away a dishevelled, tear-stained Mrs Sheridan knelt beside her husband. Price leaped from the saddle.

'Is Kit…?' he panted anxiously.

Mrs Sheridan shook her head. 'Tom, thank goodness someone's come,' relief showed in Mabel Sheridan's voice. 'Kit's been badly hit in the shoulder. He's lost a lot of blood and passed out struggling to get over here. I had to drag him most of the way.'

Price was on his knee examining the unconscious man. 'He'll be all right,' he said reassuringly. 'I'll get you both over to my place, an' get Doc Wilson from town.' He glanced at the blazing buildings. 'There's nothing we can do here. What happened, Mabel?'

'We had just started our evening meal when we realised the roof was on fire. When the men ran from the house they were shot down.'

'Did you see who it was?' asked Tom.

'When I managed to gather myself together, I saw five men driving the cattle towards the mountains,' explained Mrs Sheridan.

'Would you recognise any of them again?'

queried Price.

'No,' replied Mrs Sheridan.

'All right,' said Tom. 'Don't worry; we'll soon hev Kit seen to. It looks as if everything has gone in the fire so I'll hev to ride home an' bring back a buckboard. I should be back before it's too dark; will you be all right?'

Mrs Sheridan nodded and Tom Price was soon heading for his ranch. Once he was back at the Circle J Kit Sheridan was quickly transferred to the Running W where he was soon comfortably laid in bed.

'You're welcome to stay here as long as you like,' said Tom. 'Jest treat it as your own home.'

'We are very grateful,' replied Mrs Sheridan appreciatively.

Kit smiled his thanks. 'Who do you think did it?' he whispered.

'I'm not discussing that until Doc Wilson's seen you,' replied Tom. 'Now I've got you settled I'll ride into town.'

Tom Price hurried from the house and covered the trail to Santa Rosa at a fast gallop. He was relieved to find the doctor at home and after a brief report to the sheriff the two men quickly covered the distance to the Running W.

'You'll be all right, Kit,' reassured the doctor after he had removed the bullet and dressed the badly wounded shoulder. 'It's a matter of rest for a few days.'

'What do you think, Tom?' asked Kit after the doctor had gone. 'Rustlers?'

Tom shook his head. 'I don't know,' he replied. 'Mabel didn't get a good look at anyone, but I doubt if it's a straightforward case of rustling. I don't think rustlers would hev fired the buildings. I reckon it's all tied up with turning down these offers.'

'You mean, whoever it is, is trying to ruin us and force us to sell out,' said Kit.

'Yes,' answered Tom, 'an' of course the offers will be nowhere near as high as before.'

A worried frown creased Sheridan's forehead. 'Wal, with those cattle gone I'm as good as ruined if Farrell insists on repayment of the bank loan,' he said dejectedly.

'I'll be in the same boat if anythin' happens to mine,' said Tom. 'Another couple of days an' we'd hev hed both lots sold.'

The conversation was halted by Mrs Sheridan. 'I think you'd better get some rest, Kit,' she advised. 'A good night's sleep is what you need, and don't worry about what we are going to do, we'll deal with that later.'

Tom Price bade his friends good-night but

98

before retiring he strolled to the nearby corrals and saw that all was well with the hundred and fifty steers he was soon to sell. As he returned to the house Tom Price wished he had not given his hired hand permission to stay in town for the night. However, he reassured himself it was very unlikely that the gang would strike again so soon.

Mrs Sheridan stirred. She was still half asleep but the smell of smoke was in her nostrils. In a semi-conscious state she thought it was a nightmare but suddenly she was wide awake. It was smoke! She sat up in bed and almost at the same moment there was a pounding at the door.

'Mabel! Kit! The house is on fire!' yelled Tom.

In a flash Mrs Sheridan was out of bed and at the door. She flung it open. Tom Price stood there, half dressed, a gun in his hand. 'We've got to get out,' he shouted. 'Can you manage Kit? I'm goin' to git one of them.'

Mrs Sheridan stopped him as he turned. 'Don't go out, Tom, they'll be waiting to shoot you down, same as they did at our place.'

'Maybe you're right,' he said and hurried into another room. He peered out of the window cautiously and in the early morning light could make out three men running towards a fourth man who held their horses. Tom smashed the glass and loosed off four shots at the rustlers, but the distance was too great to be effective. An answering shot came from close at hand and the window-frame shattered close to Tom's head. He ducked below the window as three more bullets crashed into the room. Price glanced anxiously at the roof. The fire had a firm hold and sparks showered as bits of timber fell. They would have to get out and risk being shot. He hesitated a few moments before he raised himself and fired again. Tom's brain pounded; there was no return shot! He leaped to his feet and saw five riders galloping away from the blazing ranch-house driving the cattle before them.

Tom ran from the room and found Mabel and Kit coming from the bedroom.

'They've gone,' he yelled. 'Get outside, quick!'

The roof was beginning to collapse and flames were making their devouring run down the walls. The three friends hurried from the house and gulped in the fresh morning air to relieve their smoke-filled lungs. Price turned towards the stable but pulled up short when he saw that the building was also in the grip of the leaping flames. He turned slowly to his friends.

'Wal,' he muttered dejectedly, 'it looks as if they've ruined me as well.' His face hardened; his eyes blazed. 'But I'm goin' to find out who's behind this and when I do, God help him.'

'I'm with you all the way,' answered Kit grimly. 'This shoulder's painful and I feel a bit weak but I'll be all right. I'm ready to ride anytime, but where do we start? You can't possibly think thet McCoy would do this.'

Price shook his head slowly. 'I don't know, but he's behaved strangely and greed can change a man.'

'We must warn the others,' said Kit.

Tom nodded. 'You two wait here. I see some of the stable horses are not so far away.' Price hurried away and when he returned with three horses the buildings were merely smoking ruins.

Abe Carson was their nearest neighbour and both he and his wife were shocked when the three friends rode in with the news of the two raids.

'You must make your home here until things get straightened out,' pressed Mrs Carson.

'Sure,' urged Abe. 'Two extra guns will come in useful if I'm next on the list.'

'I reckon this is the time to make the association felt,' said Price. 'I reckon we should pay the others a visit.'

'Sure,' replied Abe, 'We'll form a posse an' make a search for the cattle. I'll ride with you; Kit hed better rest up fer the rest of the day.'

In spite of Sheridan's protests he had to watch his two friends ride away. By mid-morning they had formed their posse and were riding north towards the mountains. Several times they picked up cattle trails but always lost them amongst other tracks or on rougher stonier ground.

About three o'clock Tom Price called a halt. 'Reckon it's no use,' he said grimly. 'They've been too smart fer us. It must be someone who knows this country. There's one likely man thet isn't with us now and isn't fer the association.'

'You pointin' at Frank McCoy again?' snapped Mark Stevens.

'What if I am?' grunted Price.

'You know...' started Stevens.

'Cut it out, you two,' interrupted Carson sharply. 'Until we hev proof against Frank we can't take action.'

'I figure your best plan, Tom, is to ride into Santa Rosa and put the cards on the table with Farrell,' said Luke Martin. 'He might be sympathetic about your payments.'

'May be you're right,' grunted Price.

'You ride there now,' said Abe, 'an' git back to my place in time for supper.'

It was shortly before five when Tom Price rode into Santa Rosa and pulled to a halt outside the bank.

'I'm sorry to hear of this,' sympathised Farrell when Price had finished his story ten minutes later. 'You are asking me to defer the payments you and Sheridan are to make in two days' time?'

'Yes,' said Price.

Farrell looked thoughtful. 'Wal, it's a considerable sum in both cases and I'm afraid that I cannot make the final decision. I'll have to consult my superiors.'

'How long with that take?' asked Price.

'Wal as it happens, one of them is visiting Santa Rosa. I'll see him tonight and have a word for you if you come in tomorrow morning.'

Price muttered his thanks and left the bank.

Farrell watched Price from the window and once the rancher was riding down Main

Street he hurried to the Ace of Spades where he found Eugene MacCarthy in Wheeler's room. He told them of the interview with Price and when he had finished MacCarthy grinned.

'Bob Hart's worked quick and done it better than I thought,' he said. 'Wonder what he's done with the cattle? Refuse any extension of time to Sheridan and Price and tell them the bank will take over both spreads in lieu of payment. I won't be around when they ride in tomorrow; I'm goin' to visit Hart; I reckon we can speed things up.'

The following morning Eugene Mac-Carthy rode out of Santa Rosa early and made his way to the Hart gang's hide-out close to Black Water Canyon.

'Smart work, boys,' he congratulated as he swung from the saddle. 'Price and Sheridan will be on their knees after they've seen Grove Farrell today. What did you do with the cattle?'

Bob Hart grinned. 'Trust Hart to find a perfect hide-out. I'll show you later where they are. Those two raids were easy; if everything goes as easy as they did there'll be nothin' to runnin' this territory. We'll deal with Martin an' Carson next.'

'I reckon we can forget those two, and

Hardy and Briton, at any rate until we see how things develop,' said MacCarthy. He smiled at Hart's surprise and went on to explain. 'The little men have seen how we'll deal with them, so I figure if we hit one of the bigger men next, and force him to sell up, the little men will fold up and we'll get their land without any trouble.'

'Guess so,' agreed Hart. 'Who hev you in mind?'

'Mark Stevens,' replied MacCarthy. 'I hear he and the other ranchers, with the exception of McCoy, have formed an association to resist all attempts to gain their land. McCoy has refused to join them and I believe some of the ranchers are suspicious of him. That suits us by keeping their attention away from us,' he grinned.

MacCarthy spent most of the day in the mountains and it was late afternoon when he rode into Santa Rosa. After cleaning himself up he strolled over to the bank.

'Hello, Farrell,' he greeted pleasantly. 'All go well this morning?'

'Sure,' replied the bank manager. 'Thought Price was going to cut up rough but Sheridan restrained him. They took the decision rather hard but now the Circle J and Running W belong to the bank.'

'Good,' mused MacCarthy. 'The next on the list is Stevens. If he...'

MacCarthy was interrupted by a knock at the door and one of the clerks entered the room.

'Frank McCoy would like to see you,' he said.

'Tell him I'm busy at the moment,' replied Farrell.

The clerk turned to go when MacCarthy stopped him. 'No, we'll see him,' he said. 'Show him in.'

The clerk nodded and as he went back into the main office MacCarthy quickly whispered instructions to Farrell.

'Hello, McCoy,' greeted Farrell as Frank entered the office. 'I'd like you to meet Eugene MacCarthy, one of our top officials, who's here on a visit.'

The two men observed each other closely as they shook hands and exchanged greetings.

'Wal, it looks as if I might hev come at an opportune time,' said Frank as he sat down. 'It's a bad business about Kit Sheridan and Tom Price,' he went on. 'I heard this afternoon thet you can't extend repayment time for them and thet the bank has taken over both ranches.'

'Thet's so,' replied Farrell.

MacCarthy smiled. 'It does seem hard on them but certain policies have been laid down by my colleagues which make any extension out of the question.'

Frank nodded. 'I see,' he said. 'Then are these ranches up for sale?'

'I don't think...' began Farrell.

'Just a minute, Grove,' interrupted Mac-Carthy. 'Am I to understand you want to buy them?'

'Not both,' replied Frank. 'I'm interested in Sheridan's spread, it joins up to my land and I could easily work it all together.'

'You're becoming rather a big landowner,' said MacCarthy, 'Aren't you afraid being hit like Sheridan and Price?'

'I figure thet I'm in a much stronger position to resist any attacks,' answered Frank, 'besides we'll git these rustlers in time, sheriff's out lookin' now.'

'If you think it wise to expand at a time like this,' said MacCarthy, 'you can have the Circle J.' He turned to Farrell. 'Make the necessary arrangements, Grove.' He caught the surprised look of annoyance on Farrell's face.

'Thanks,' said Frank rising to his feet. 'I'll collect the deeds in the morning.'

As the door shut behind McCoy, Farrell turned on MacCarthy angrily. 'What's this idea?' he snapped, his eyes blazing.

MacCarthy's jaw tightened. 'Who are you questioning?'

'I figured thet in all this land buying there might be one piece thet I could hev, especially after all I've done,' rapped Farrell. 'The Circle J is just the place I want.'

'Jumping to conclusions, aren't you?' snapped MacCarthy. 'I'm running this show.' His eyes were cold as he stared at Farrell. 'Don't get big ideas,' he added. 'If you get out of line it will be too bad for you. You'll get your payment all in good time.'

'But why sell to the opposition?' Anger still showed in Farrell's voice.

'When it comes to playing it big you can't see very far,' sneered MacCarthy. 'You know thet some of the ranchers think McCoy is behind all this land buying – well when they hear of this they'll be even more convinced and it's diverting suspicion from us. We'll git the Circle J back all in good time but first we deal with Mark Stevens.'

Chapter Seven

Bob Hart and his gang watched the first light of day reveal a herd of five hundred cattle grazing peacefully in a wide bowl-shaped hollow on Mark Stevens' ranch. As they lay in the long grass on the edge of the hollow Hart studied the herd carefully.

'MacCarthy told me this herd is due to be shipped tomorrow,' he whispered. 'If we git it Stevens will be hit pretty hard.' He paused a moment. 'There are only four men watching this herd. We'll hit it from this side, Russ an' Wade straight at it, Jake an' Red on either side – if we funnel those beeves straight over the other side of the hollow we'll be headin' fer the mountains.' He looked at his men and they each nodded their understanding. 'I'll be around to lend a hand where necessary. All right git to the horses; I'll give the signal when to ride.'

The four men crept away from the rim of the hollow before rising to their feet and hurrying to their horses which were picketed a short distance away.

Bob watched the riders circling the herd in the hollow. He saw that two of them would meet on the side of the herd nearest to him whilst the other two would be at the far side. He guessed they would pause for a chat, maybe light a cigarette, so he waved to his men who trotted forward bringing his horse with them. Bob moved away from the hollow before jumping to his feet and running to his horse. He leaped into the saddle and the five men kicked their horses forward and burst into the hollow at full gallop. Surprised by the sudden pound of hooves the two cowboys turned in the saddles and were startled to see five men, with guns drawn, hurtling towards them. They tugged at their Colts but almost before the guns had left the leather they were cut down by the whining bullets. The steers, frightened by the thundering hooves and crashing gunfire, started to move away from the disturbance. Jake and Red were already riding alongside the herd and, with Wade, Russ and Bob urging the steers forward, there was only one way for them to turn. The two cowboys on the far side of the herd spurred their horses in an attempt to ride across the herd and prevent the cattle from running but, almost before they realised what was happening, the stampeding steers were on top of them. The horses screamed as horns ripped into their flesh. They turned and tried to run before the surge of bellowing animals but in their terror they lost their footing, pitching their riders to a death under the trampling, unmerciful hooves of the herd.

As soon as he saw the cattle were heading in the right direction Bob Hart swung out from behind the herd. He realised that the stampede must be controlled and he urged his horse into full gallop alongside the steers. Gradually he out-rode the herd and pulled across the front of the cattle riding back and forth. When Jake and Red saw their leader ride ahead they moved in closer to the leading steers pressing them inwards helping Bob in his attempt to slow down the pace. Gradually the herd came under control and settled down to a speed dictated by the outlaws.

As the herd pounded across the grassland a figure stirred in the hollow. The cowboy pushed himself to his knees with his sound arm, the other hung limp from a shattered shoulder and blood oozed from a wound in his side. He gazed for a moment at his dead companion, then struggled slowly to his feet. He swayed, staggered forward a few steps and then pulled up sharply, horrified at the sight of the trampled, almost unrecognisable remains of men and horses. His legs buckled bringing him to his knees, and he retched at the sickening sight before him. When his head began to clear a few minutes later he looked around, and was relieved to see his horse standing on one side of the hollow. The cowboy gave a low whistle and the animal, pricking up its ears, gave a low whinny and walked slowly towards him. When the horse stopped beside him the man reached upwards, grasped the stirrup and pulled himself to his feet. The effort drained a lot of his energy and he stood for a few moments leaning against the side of the horse. Glancing round he saw the dust from the herd billowing upwards across the grassland and the sight of it seemed to add new life to him. He grasped the saddle horn with his sound arm and with an effort, which caused pain in his side, managed to get one foot into the stirrup. His face creased with pain, he pulled himself upwards and succeeded in swinging into the saddle. The effort was so great that he almost fainted but, steadying himself, he sat for a few moments whilst he regained some strength.

He sent his mount forward at a slow walk

and left the hollow in the direction taken by the outlaws. The dust cloud, indicating the progress of the herd, was far across the grassland. He put his horse into a gentle trot but, before long, he realised that he was weakening fast and would not be able to stand much more riding. He slowed the animal back to a walking pace and soon knew that it was useless to try to follow the stolen cattle any longer. He halted and watched the dust cloud for some time before he saw it swing to the right.

'Headin' fer Black Water Canyon area,' he gasped. 'Frank McCoy's land!'

He pulled the horse round and headed for the Swinging L.

Mark Stevens and his foreman Tay Walsh were checking a herd of horses about a mile from the house when the foreman drew his attention to a lone horseman, who was moving at a slow pace across the grassland. They watched him for a few moments and then, seeing the man sway in the saddle, they put their horses into a gallop towards him.

'Jess Sinclair!' gasped Walsh as they neared the rider.

'Should be with the herd,' yelled Mark. 'Something's wrong.'

They pulled their horses alongside Sinclair

and supported him in the saddle. He glanced up and a look of relief came into his eyes when he recognised the two men.

'Made it, thank goodness,' he gasped.

'What happened?' asked Mark anxiously.

'Cattle gone ... other three killed...' The words were scarcely above a whisper.

'What!' Mark gasped.

'Guess they thought I was dead,' panted Sinclair. He slumped forward and would have fallen out of the saddle but for the support of the two men.

'Let's git him out of the saddle,' said Mark.

The two men soon had the cowboy, his head supported by his saddle, laid on the ground. His eyes flickered open as Tay Walsh forced some water between his lips.

'Tay, ride back to the house,' instructed Mark, 'Send one of the men fer Doc Wilson an' bring the buggy back here, we'll need it to git Jess back to the ranch.'

Walsh was about to move when Sinclair stopped him. He turned his head towards Mark. 'Thanks, boss, but it's no use, I'm finished.' He paused, and indicated he wanted another drink.

'Nonsense,' said Mark emphatically as Tay gave the wounded man another drink.

'You'll be all right once the doc sees you.'
He nodded to Tay who climbed to his feet.

'Wait,' gasped Jess. 'Let me finish. There were four of them … took us by surprise.'

'Did you recognise them?' asked Mark.

'Couldn't, boss,' answered Jess. 'They hed neckerchiefs over their faces but I followed them so far … they headed fer the Black Water Canyon area – Frank McCoy's land!'

Mark shot a quick glance at his foreman whose face remained impassive at the news. Before Mark could say anything Jess reached for another drink. The ranch owner nodded to his foreman who hurried off without a word as Sinclair wet his lips again.

Half an hour later Tay Walsh was back with the buggy.

'How is he, boss?' he asked as he jumped to the ground.

'Very weak,' replied Mark. 'He hasn't spoken again since you left.'

The two men lifted the wounded man gently into the wagon and after tying the two saddle horses to the back Mark took the reins whilst Tay stayed beside Jess.

'The doc should be there almost as soon as we are,' said Tay, and Mark sent the horses slowly forward.

They had covered about half the distance

to the ranch when Tay scrambled over to sit beside Mark. 'I'm afraid he's gone, boss,' he muttered sadly.

Mark stared at him almost disbelievingly for a moment. His eyes narrowed slowly; his jaw tightened. 'Four good men murdered,' he muttered between tight lips. 'Someone's goin' to pay dearly fer this!'

The two men rode on in silence until Tay reluctantly broke it. 'Boss ... I know ... what do you...' he stuttered trying hard to put his thoughts into words. 'What about Jess seeing those steers being driven on to McCoy's land?' The words suddenly poured from his lips.

Mark pulled the horses to a halt and turned to face his foreman. 'Tay, you don't believe Frank is behind this?' he said. His voice showed that he was surprised that his foreman should entertain such a thought.

'But others think he is,' pointed out Walsh, 'an' from what I gather there's some evidence stacked against McCoy. Now, with what Jess saw it looks mighty like...'

'Only you an' I know what Jess saw.' Mark's voice was cold. 'I don't...' he stopped; his brain pounded as he stared at his foreman. 'You didn't tell anyone back at the ranch what Jess said?' asked Mark anxiously.

The foreman shook his head. 'No, didn't give it a thought I was in too big a hurry to get back here.'

'Good,' said Mark, relief showing in his voice.

'But, boss,' protested Walsh, 'you can't ignore it.'

'I don't intend to,' replied Mark. 'Frank's been too good a friend for me to go around accusing him without evidence.'

'But Jess saw the cattle moving into the Black Water Canyon area,' insisted Tay. 'Sheridan's an' Price's cattle are probably somewhere there as well. With all those beeves on his land McCoy must know about them.'

'I happen to know that Frank hasn't been up in Black Water Canyon lately,' rapped Mark.

'Boss, you aren't with him all the time,' replied Tay. 'Loyalty is all very well, but men hev been murdered.'

Anger flared in Mark's eyes. 'There's been enough said,' snapped Mark. 'I don't intend to let the murderers escape.' He jerked the reins hard sending the horses forward. Tay knew that it was best to say no more to his boss and the rest of the journey was made in silence.

When Doc Wilson arrived at the Swinging L Mark Stevens hurried to meet him. 'Sorry, Doc,' he said. 'I'm afraid it's too late; Jess died on the way back here.'

The doctor offered his sympathies and after examining the body returned to town.

It was around noon when Mark Stevens and his foreman were talking on the verandah of the house when Grove Farrell rode up.

'Hello, Farrell,' greeted Mark, 'it's not often you ride this way.'

'Wal, I heard in town about what happened this morning,' said Farrell without dismounting. 'I'm sorry you've been hit so hard,' he went on, 'but I'll still expect you the day after tomorrow with a payment on thet loan.'

Mark's face hardened. He glanced at Tay and saw his eyes narrow angrily and it pleased Mark to know that his foreman had not taken their argument on the range too harshly.

'But, Farrell, surely under the circumstances you'll grant me an extension,' said Mark, 'I was relying on the money I was going to get for the cattle.'

'I'm sorry, Stevens,' replied Farrell. 'It's entirely out of my hands. I've had instructions to make a transfer of cash to the office in Denver, and I need thet money from you.' He looked hard at Mark. 'Just see that it's there or you'll say goodbye to this lot.' He pulled his horse round and rode away.

Fire blazed in Walsh's eyes. 'The little, sneaking... I'll smash...'

'Take it easy, Tay,' said Mark calmly. 'I'd like to do thet, but it wouldn't do any good.' He shrugged his shoulders. 'I'm in a tight spot, Tay.' He paced up and down for a few moments.

'How about the horses,' suggested Tay. 'Can't you push the sale forward?'

''Fraid not,' replied Mark. 'I can't ship them until next week an' thet will be too late.' He strode off the verandah and swung on to his horse. 'I'm goin' to pay Frank a visit,' he said. 'Keep an eye on things, especially those horses.'

Walsh nodded and watched his boss ride away in the direction of the Lazy A.

Frank McCoy was examining some cattle when the sound of a galloping horse caught his attention.

'Something wrong, Mark?' called Frank when he saw the serious look on his friend's face.

'Sure is,' replied Mark swinging out of the

119

saddle. 'Four men killed an' five hundred head of cattle gone!'

'What!' Frank gasped.

Mark went on to relate the happenings of the early morning.

'Did Jess have any idea who they were?' asked Frank when Mark concluded his story.

'No,' replied Mark. He paused, looking at the ground thoughtfully, a frown creasing his forehead. 'But there was something.' Mark looked up and stared straight at Frank. 'The last time Jess saw those cattle they were being driven on to your land in the Black Water Canyon area!'

Frank was taken aback by the inference of this statement. He matched look for look. 'You don't think I'm behind these raids, do you?' he asked coldly.

Mark hesitated. Suddenly the tension went out of him. 'No, of course not, Frank,' he replied emphatically. 'But I'm worried about what the others will think; these things hev a habit of getting out.'

Frank looked thoughtful. 'You're right, Mark,' he said. 'As a matter of fact I should hev joined the association right at the start, guess I'd better join now, then no one need hev any more suspicions about me an' we can start lookin' fer the real brains behind all this.'

'I reckon your joining now wouldn't convince some of them,' replied Mark. 'Price would say you were doing it as a blind. An' when they hear about my cattle, things could git pretty ugly. I figure it might be wisest if you were out of the way fer a few days.'

'I'm not fer runnin' away,' rapped Frank. 'Thet would make them even more suspicious.' He paused for a moment. 'Wait a minute; let them think what they like. I've been planning a trip up Black Water Canyon; if I go now I can scout round fer the steers.'

'Good idea,' agreed Mark.

'Right, now we've got to settle about your payment to the bank,' said Frank. 'It's struck me as strange that these rustlings should take place just before payments hev been due; it would seem as if the rustlers knew an' were actin' on information.'

'You don't think Grove Farrell...' started Mark.

'I reckon he's in the setup somewhere,' cut in Frank, 'but I can't see him being the brains behind the whole thing. I figure if you make this payment to the bank, Farrell and whoever is behind him will git a shock. It's goin' to upset their plans an' maybe force their hand.'

'You could be right,' agreed Stevens, 'but where am I goin' to git the money?'

'I'll lend it to you,' replied Frank.

'Thet's mighty kind,' answered Mark. 'After the way you helped me revive the old ranch when Gloria took it over from her father and now this, I'll never be out of your debt.'

'Nonsense,' said Frank with a grin.

'I'll be able to pay you back fairly soon,' said Mark. 'I'm selling a herd of my best horses next week.'

'Take care they aren't rustled,' advised Frank.

'I sure will,' said Mark. 'I'm goin' to move them to Rainbow Gulch. With only one entrance one man can guard them an' they should be safe there, beside no one outside of my men will know that they are there.'

'Thet's a good idea,' agreed Frank. 'C'm on in, Mark, I'll git you the money. It will be more effective if you pay Farrell in cash, but don't let him know it came from me.'

Chapter Eight

Grove Farrell had mixed thoughts as he watched the door close behind Mark Stevens. He had controlled his astonishment when Stevens had walked in and payed off the money due in two days' time. He gave Stevens a few minutes to get clear of the bank before picking up his sombrero and hurrying across to the Ace of Spades. A few minutes later he had confronted MacCarthy and Wheeler with the latest developments.

'You've slipped up somewhere, Farrell,' snarled MacCarthy, annoyed at the setback to his plans. 'You reckoned this raid would bring Stevens to his knees.'

'How was I to know he'd hev thet amount of cash at home?' snapped Farrell.

'Maybe he borrowed it,' pointed out Wheeler.

'Well, we're goin' to have to think again,' said MacCarthy. 'Come on, Wheeler, you and I will take a ride over Stevens' spread and figure out the next move.'

Little over an hour later the two men

123

pulled their horses to a sudden halt as they topped a small rise on Swinging L land.

'Thet's a mighty fine herd of horses,' observed MacCarthy. 'Who's that moving them?'

'Mark Stevens and two of his men,' answered Wheeler as he watched the herd being skilfully handled.

'They aren't heading for the ranch,' pointed out MacCarthy. 'They may be worth following.'

Throughout the afternoon the two men leisurely followed the herd which was heading towards the mountains.

'They're putting them into Rainbow Gulch,' said Wheeler as they watched from the cover of some boulders. 'Looks as if Stevens is takin' precautions with this lot.' He grinned. 'But he's played into our hands. There's only one entrance to the Gulch, should be easy for Bob Hart to rustle thet lot.'

MacCarthy looked thoughtful. 'I reckon we can kill two birds with one stone,' he said. 'We'll rustle those horses and drive some of them on to Frank McCoy's land, mix them with his horses an' thet, on top of everything else, should really convince the other ranchers that McCoy is behind these raids.'

'Smart work,' agreed Wheeler.

'It's going to need careful planning,' warned MacCarthy. He was thoughtful for a while as they watched Stevens and his men herding the horses into the gulch. Suddenly he turned to Wheeler. 'Floyd, I want you to ride back to town,' he instructed. 'Tell Farrell to call a meeting of the ranchers for tomorrow morning, ten thirty. I'm going to wait here and see what guard Stevens leave, then I'll ride to see Hart and put him wise to my plans.'

Wheeler nodded, hurried to his horse and headed for Santa Rosa.

The following morning Bob Hart and his gang halted their horses close to Rainbow Gulch. Bob and Jake slipped from the saddles and moved forward stealthily on foot. Near the entrance to the gulch they saw a cowboy, leaning against some rocks, rolling himself a cigarette.

'I'll take him,' whispered Bob. 'Keep me covered but fire if he gets the drop on me. We've got to do this without a killing if possible.'

Jake nodded and both men drew their Colts. Bob crept forward stealthily, until he was about three yards from the unsuspecting man. Suddenly he leaped to his feet and flung himself forward, bringing the barrel of his Colt crashing down on the man's head. The cowboy pitched to the ground without a groan. Bob watched him for a moment before turning to wave to Jake who in turn signalled to the other three outlaws. When the men reached him Bob issued his instructions quickly.

'Red, Jake,' he said, 'drive the horses out of the Gulch. Russ, Wade, cut out the first twenty-five or so, head them for McCoy's spread an' put them with his herd. I'll help Red to take the rest to our hideout. Jake, you will stay with our friend here,' he added nodding to the unconscious man, 'an' see that he doesn't leave here before ten. MacCarthy wants him to reach town during the meeting he's arranged.'

The men nodded, pulled their neckerchiefs over their faces and moved off to carry out their leader's instructions.

Eugene MacCarthy glanced at his watch. 'Twenty past ten,' he said. 'They should be riding in soon.' Floyd Wheeler moved closer to the window from which he could see the main street. 'By the way, Floyd,' went on MacCarthy, 'has Butch Lant had anything to report?'

'No,' replied Wheeler. 'He's been keeping a close tag on Farrell, but he's done nothing to rouse Butch's suspicions.'

'Good,' replied MacCarthy, 'but tell Butch not to ease his vigilance; Farrell doesn't like the hold we have over him and he was cut up when I told him to sell McCoy the Circle J.'

'Here's the first of them,' called Wheeler when Abe Carson pulled to a halt in front of the bank. A few minutes later Wheeler reported the arrival of Kit Sheridan and Tom Price. It was close on half past ten when Wes Briton arrived with Luke Martin.

'Wal I guess I'll be getting across to the bank,' said MacCarthy and, as he reached the door, Wheeler informed him that Mark Stevens and George Hardy had arrived.

'Then, that just leaves McCoy,' mused MacCarthy as he left the Ace of Spades.

A few minutes later he entered Grove Farrell's office where the ranchers were standing in three groups. When Farrell saw MacCarthy come in he excused himself from Mark Stevens and went to meet him. After they had exchanged greetings Farrell called to the ranchers.

'Gentlemen, please sit down.'

The ranchers shuffled into their places

127

whilst MacCarthy and Farrell made their way to the two chairs at the other side of the big desk. When everyone was settled Farrell addressed the men in front of him.

'Gentlemen,' he said, 'I want to introduce Mister Eugene MacCarthy to you. Mister MacCarthy is one of our high officials who is visiting us for a few days and, in view of recent, unfortunate events, he thought it might be a good idea if he had a word with you and explained the bank's position.'

MacCarthy rose to his feet. 'I'm very pleased to make the acquaintance of you gentlemen,' he said smoothly. 'I understand that one of you is not here, but as he is the biggest and most powerful landowner and rancher around here maybe he isn't affected the same as the rest of you.'

MacCarthy smiled to himself when he saw Price's face darken at this reference to McCoy and saw him whisper something to Sheridan. He figured the seed had been sown and that if everything went as planned McCoy would be in trouble. 'It is unfortunate that this rustling should have taken place at this time,' MacCarthy went on. 'Normally the bank would have been pleased to help you out of your difficulties and extend the repayment period, but at this moment there are certain schemes being carried out back east which prevents us from extending the loan periods. We need all the money we can get and whilst we don't like taking your land in lieu of payment it is the only course open to us. I'm sorry, gentlemen, but there it is.'

A buzz of conversation broke out as MacCarthy sat down, and continued for a few moments until the scraping of a chair caused everyone to turn to see Tom Price rising to his feet.

'Mister MacCarthy, we appreciate your point,' he said in his bustling manner, 'but it doesn't help our problem any. Stevens was lucky enough to be able to pay you but if he's hit again or if any of the others are hit then they'll be in the same boat as Kit Sheridan and myself.'

'Have you any suggestions about what should be done?' asked MacCarthy.

'Shore,' answered Price. 'We've already formed ourselves into an association an' if I'd hed my way we'd hev taken more positive action before now.'

'We've searched an' found no trace of your cattle,' called out Mark Stevens.

'I'm not talking about mere searches,' retorted Price. 'If we'd hev acted on our first suspicions maybe Kit and I would hev still hed our spreads.'

'You'd nothin' to go on,' snapped Mark. 'You'd hev looked a fool.'

Price ignored his remark and turned his attention back to MacCarthy.

'Before you came here,' he said, 'there hed been a great deal of purchasing of land. We figure whoever did thet is now trying to git hold of our ranches. If he forces us to give them up he'll probably come to you wantin' to buy them. You can help us by telling us who was responsible for the original purchasing of land and if thet person has approached you in order to buy either mine or Sheridan's?'

When Price finished everyone started talking at once. Farrell looked sharply at MacCarthy who watched the ranchers for a moment before he spoke.

'You believe in coming to the point, Price,' smiled MacCarthy, 'but really, you are asking an awful lot of us; after all, banking matters are confidential.'

'But surely when the situation is desperate, you can do something,' shouted Luke Martin.

'If you know anything tell us,' called Wes Briton.

130

'Gentlemen, please,' called MacCarthy raising his hands for silence. 'Price,' he went on, 'from what I hear you've been suspicious of someone all the time, might I ask who it is?'

'Frank McCoy!' answered Price.

'Impossible!' yelled Mark Stevens jumping to his feet and glaring angrily at Price. 'A straighter man you never met, our ex-sheriff, he is...'

'Thet don't mean he can't go wrong,' cut in Sheridan.

'McCoy isn't here this morning to speak for himself,' said MacCarthy, pleased at the way things were turning out. 'Is he a member of your association?'

'No,' answered Price. 'Said it wasn't necessary.'

'I saw him yesterday and he agreed he had been wrong in the first place and said he would join the association now,' rapped Mark.

Price laughed raucously. 'He sure can pull the wool over your eyes, Mark, thet's just a blind to cover these other activities.'

'If he wanted to join us why isn't he here now,' shouted Abe Carson.

'He was talking of going into Black Water Canyon hoping to get a lead on the rustlers;

maybe he's already gone,' snapped Mark and almost before the words were out he realised he had made a mistake in telling them of Frank's whereabouts.

'There you are,' yelled Price. 'Black Water Canyon. I hear thet's where your cowpoke saw your steers being driven; seems your precious Frank McCoy's goin' to look them over. It just adds strength to our suspicions.' Mark did not answer and Price turned to MacCarthy. 'Wal, can you tell us anything or not?' he asked.

MacCarthy hesitated for a moment. 'Wal,' he said, 'regarding the first buying I can't help you there, we received instructions in a roundabout way but in view of all the circumstances I think it best to tell you that McCoy has purchased the Circle J!'

'What!' Sheridan leaped to his feet. 'Thet's enough for me, McCoy's our man!'

'Hold it!' Mark was on his feet. 'Thet doesn't prove anything. Has he purchased Price's spread?'

'No,' replied MacCarthy. 'The bank still holds it.'

'If he is behind all this land buying he'd hev bought thet as well,' shouted Mark.

Price laughed. 'Jest another cover,' he yelled, 'but he won't get away with it.'

Men were on their feet all shouting at the same time. Things had gone better than MacCarthy had expected and all that was needed was for the report to come in from the range. He glanced anxiously at his watch. If Hart had carried out his part of the plan then the cowboy should be riding in at any moment. At all costs he must keep these ranchers a little longer.

'Gentlemen, gentlemen,' he yelled above the noise. 'It's no good rushing after McCoy now, you heard that he'd headed for Black Water Canyon. Just calm down; I've laid on some drinks here and I'd hoped to meet you all personally. Grove, get our friends a drink.'

As his neighbours accepted the offer Mark Stevens turned disgustedly to the door. MacCarthy saw him and hurried to detain him.

'Stevens,' he said. 'Don't take this too hard; things have to be proved yet.' He heard the sound of a galloping horse as he spoke and a few moments later the door of the office burst open. Everyone spun round to face the door and silence fell upon the room when they saw a dust-covered, dishevelled, breathless cowboy standing there.

For a moment Mark was stunned by this unexpected arrival then suddenly he moved forward to face the man. 'What's happened, Del?' he asked anxiously.

There was some measure of relief in the man's eyes when he saw Mark. 'I was jumped, Boss, the horses rustled,' he panted.

'What!' Mark gasped. 'But we've only just moved them. When did it happen?' A buzz of amazement went round the room but ceased when Del spoke again.

'This morning,' he said, 'I never knew what hit me. When I came to, the horses had gone an' some masked hombre was guarding me.'

'Masked!' MacCarthy sounded surprised as if the word brought back some memory. 'I saw two masked men driving some horses on McCoy's spread when I was out riding this morning,' he went on. 'I thought they had tied their neckerchiefs round their faces because of the dust.'

Pandemonium broke out at the implications of MacCarthy's statement. Mark was speechless.

'McCoy again,' shouted Price. 'This settles it.'

'You said you'd just moved these horses,' said MacCarthy. 'Did you tell anyone you were going to move them?'

'Only my men,' answered Mark.

'What about McCoy?' asked MacCarthy.

Mark shook his head but suddenly doubt showed in his eyes as he realised that he had told his friend.

'I see you did,' said MacCarthy, quick to seize on the opportunity. 'Looks pretty bad for McCoy.'

'Boss, there's one thing more,' said Del. 'This hombre thet was guarding me kept looking at his watch. At ten o'clock he said, "Ten, time I was ridin'." He cut my hands free an' told me to clear out when I'd got my legs untied. He warned me not to follow or I'd be shot down. However, when I was free I followed but he'd had a good start and I soon lost sight of him. Then someone fired at me. It wasn't a healthy place to be so I high-tailed back to the ranch where I learned you were here.' The man paused a moment then added emphatically, 'Boss, when I followed thet hombre he was heading fer McCoy's spread!'

'There's only one thing to do,' yelled Price, 'ride out there an' find out.'

The other ranchers yelled their agreement and everyone hurried outside. Dust swirled as the ranchers accompanied by MacCarthy and Farrell headed for the Lazy A at an earth pounding gallop.

Once they reached Lazy A land Mac-

Carthy led the way to the place where he had seen the horses. They slowed their gallop and approached the animals cautiously until MacCarthy called a halt.

'Reckon we'll wait here and let Stevens and Price go ahead,' he said.

The two men moved forward and a few moments later Price called out. 'Swinging L brand here.' There was almost a note of triumph in his voice.

Mark's brain pounded as he rode back to the group of ranchers to whom he had to admit that there were some of his horses amongst Frank's.

'We'll pay clever Mister McCoy a visit,' shouted Price, 'maybe he hasn't left for Black Water Canyon yet.'

The group of men turned their horses and before long they were pulling to a halt outside the lazy A ranch-house where Frank's wife alarmed at the pounding of hooves was on the verandah to meet them.

'Mornin' ma'am,' greeted MacCarthy. 'Is your husband at home?'

Abigail McCoy looked anxiously at the group of men. 'Sorry, he's gone up to Black Water Canyon. Is anything wrong?'

'Some of my horses have been rustled, Abbe,' began Mark.

'We needn't worry Mrs McCoy with the details, Stevens,' cut in MacCarthy hastily. 'When is your husband likely to be back, ma'am.'

'I don't know,' replied Abbe. 'Maybe two or three days.'

'Tell him we'd like to see him when he returns,' said MacCarthy. 'C'm on, we'll get back to town.'

The men turned their horses. Abigail saw Mark hesitate and glance at her but a muttered word from Price caused him to move away with the others.

Once out of sight of the ranch-house Mac-Carthy called a halt. 'I reckon a watch ought to be kept on the house,' he suggested.

'A good idea,' agreed Price.

'I'll arrange for three of my men to do it in shifts,' said Abe Carson.

'Right,' said Price. 'I'll stay here until the first one comes, you never know if Mrs McCoy was foolin' us. There are some boulders a short way back, just off the trail; they'll be a good place from which to watch the house.'

Price rode off to take up his position whilst the rest of the ranchers headed for the respective spreads. MacCarthy and Farrell headed for town congratulating themselves on the way things had turned out.

'McCoy's a dead duck,' grinned Mac-Carthy, 'and when this lot are through with him his ranch will be ripe for the picking and then it will be easy to fold up the rest of them.'

He would not have been so smug if he had known that at that moment Mark Stevens was turning his horse to head back to the Lazy A.

Mark's thoughts had troubled him as he rode towards his ranch. So much evidence pointed at Frank and yet it pointed a little too conveniently. Mark stopped.

He rubbed his chin thoughtfully. 'I guess the best thing is to contact Frank,' he muttered. 'Maybe Abbe…' he pulled his horse round and headed for the Lazy A.

Slipping off the trail before reaching Price's look-out point Mark approached it on foot. He pulled his neckerchief over his face and crept stealthily forward. Price never knew what hit him and Mark soon had the unconscious man bound and gagged. He hurried back to his horse and galloped for the Lazy A.

The pounding hooves brought Abbe hurrying on to the verandah and relief showed in her face when she saw Mark. He leaped from the saddle and hurried inside with Abigail.

'There's something desperately wrong, isn't there?' said Abbe. 'I guessed it when you were all here before.'

Mark quickly explained the situation to her. 'Things look black for Frank,' he concluded, 'but there's something strange about the whole setup. We must contact Frank and I must be away from here before Abe Carson's man arrives and finds Price.'

'I'll try to find Frank,' suggested Abbe.

'If you aren't seen around here, they'll be suspicious,' pointed out Mark, 'an' I can't be missing. We must keep things looking normal around here.'

'Who can we send?' asked Abbe anxiously.

'I don't...' Mark's words were interrupted by a loud knock at the front door. Abbe looked anxiously at Mark. 'Better see who it is,' said Mark. 'If it's Price, then Abe Carson's man has got here quicker than I expected. Let them in an let me do the talkin'.'

Abbe hurried from the room and crossed the hall. Opening the front door she saw two, dust-covered, weather-beaten, leather-faced men of about fifty. As soon as they saw her they removed their battered hats.

'Hello, Abbe,' said one of them.

Abigail stared for a moment. 'Clint! Clint

Schofield!' she gasped incredulously suddenly recognising the speaker.

Broad smiles split both their faces.

'Told you she'd remember me,' said Clint. 'Abbe, this is Zeke Dolan.'

'Pleased to meet you,' replied Abbe. 'Come in.' As she closed the door behind them she asked, 'What brings you up here?'

'Gold,' replied Clint. 'Zeke here has a map showing thet there's gold in Black Water Canyon.'

'Black Water Canyon!' Abbe gasped. 'That's Frank's land; he's up there now. Are you...' she stopped suddenly. Her mind was racing quickly. 'You've come just at the right time, you're the answer to our problem,' she said excitedly. She led the way into the room where she introduced Mark Stevens who quickly told the two men of the troubles around Santa Rosa.

'If you're heading for Black Water Canyon you can carry the message to Frank,' concluded Mark. 'No one will suspect you. But you must go straight away; thet cowboy will be at thet lookout point very soon.'

'Please do it, Clint,' begged Abbe.

Clint patted her on the shoulder. 'Of course we'll do it, only too pleased to. We'd figured on staying around here a couple of

140

days, but we'll do thet on our way back.' He smiled at Abbe. 'And don't worry,' he comforted, 'everything will be all right.'

The three men hurried from the house and left at a brisk gallop. Once out of sight of the ranch Mark bade them goodbye and swung round to the lookout point where he made sure they had not been seen leaving the Lazy A.

Chapter Nine

The two prospectors rode hard but they failed to make contact with Frank before dark.

The following morning after a good breakfast they moved further into the mountains and were soon heading along Black Water Canyon. After about an hour's steady progress the two men rounded a spur in the cliff and saw Frank examining the ground a short distance ahead.

The sound of the horses' hooves on the hard ground caused Frank to straighten sharply; his hand flying to his holster.

Frank's hand froze on the butt of his Colt.

His eyes narrowed, scanning the two men who were obviously prospectors. Suddenly his eyes widened with surprise as the men came nearer and he recognised Clint.

'Clint!' he yelled and ran forward to meet him.

The two men pulled their horses to a halt and climbed from the saddles.

'What on earth are you doin' here?' asked Frank, grasping Clint's hand firmly.

'Gold,' replied Clint with a grin.

'Gold?' said Frank in amazement. 'There's no gold up here.'

'According to Zeke there is,' answered Clint.

Frank and Zeke exchanged greetings and Zeke briefly explained about the map.

'Wal, you're at liberty to search,' said Frank.

'Thanks,' replied Clint. 'It seems we've arrived at an opportune time; you appear to be in a heap of trouble.'

'Wal, it's not that bad,' said Frank with a grin.

'Seems things hev got worse since you left home,' said Clint who went on to explain the latest developments.

Before Clint had finished there was a worried look on Frank's face.

'I must get back at once,' he said when Clint finished his story. 'The clues to this whole business lie in the bank and in these mountains. Cattle and horses can't disappear into thin air. Will you two continue the search whilst I go back?'

Reassured by the two men that they would do everything possible, Frank mounted his horse and headed out of the canyon unaware that the meeting and departure had been watched by two men high up on the canyon's rim.

Deciding that it would be unwise to return to the Lazy A whilst it was being watched Frank kept to a fast pace towards the Swinging L. There were no cowboys about when he approached the ranch but two horses were hitched to the rail outside the house. He slowed to a walking pace, alert and tense in the saddle. He swung from the leather and stepped on to the verandah when Tay Walsh came round the corner of the building. Tay stopped sharply in his tracks, his hand flying to his holster but Frank was quicker and Tay found himself staring at the cold muzzle of a Colt before his own weapon was half out of its holster.

'Leave it, Tay,' snapped Frank.

Tay let the gun drop back into place and

moved his hand away from its butt.

'Mark in?' asked Frank.

'Sure,' nodded the Swinging L foreman. 'The men have ridden out to the range an' we were about to follow.'

'All right, inside,' said Frank motioning towards the door with his gun.

Tay stepped forward, opened the door and with the gun pointing at his back walked inside. Mark stared in amazement as the two men entered the house.

'What's this?' he asked incredulously.

'Tay tried to outdraw me,' replied Frank.

'Sorry, boss,' said Walsh. 'It was automatic reaction at seeing McCoy an' knowin' about the horses.'

'Thet's all right,' said Frank, giving the foreman a friendly pat on the shoulder.

The foreman smiled and left the house. 'Thanks fer getting word to me by Clint and Zeke,' said Frank as the door closed.

'Glad they found you so soon,' replied Mark. 'What do you figure on doin' now?'

'I've got to prove thet I've nothin' to do with it,' answered Frank.

'But how?' asked Mark. 'You must admit thet things look pretty black for you an' there's some justification fer the other ranchers thinking as they do.'

Frank nodded. 'I guess you're right.' He looked thoughtful. 'I've been doin' some hard thinkin' on my way here. I figure thet someone is tryin' to take over this territory. When all thet land was bought I reckoned some syndicate was behind it – I'm not so sure now. When we turned down the offers to sell out a gang was organised to carry out these raids to try to intimidate us. They hit two small men an' then figured if they crippled someone bigger the others would sell out. They tried you, but when you made your payment they stole your horses, and tried to ruin me by throwing the blame my way.'

'It would add up thet way,' agreed Mark. 'Then it must be someone who knows this territory, they obviously know the mountains, an' someone who knows our affairs; we were all raided at vital times.'

'Yes,' replied Frank. 'An' thet points to Grove Farrell.'

'Farrell!' gasped Mark. 'But he couldn't operate on a scale like this.'

'He has the knowledge,' pointed out Frank. 'He could have a partner, maybe Wheeler.'

'Wait a minute,' cried Mark. Excitement showed in his eyes. 'What about this stranger, Eugene MacCarthy? These raids

145

started after he arrived; Farrell could hev acted for him previously.'

'You could be right,' said Frank eagerly. 'Clint an' Zeke are goin' to search fer a lead in the mountains; I'm goin' to town to see if I can get a lead through the bank.'

'Is it wise fer you to go?' queried Mark. 'The way this thing's built up there are several people would like to see you behind bars.'

Frank smiled. 'I know,' he said. 'I'll be careful; I'll wait here until it's nearly dark if you don't mind.'

Darkness was creeping across the countryside when Frank McCoy approached Santa Rosa. As he neared the town he turned on to a side trail and entered the town by a back street. He rode slowly, his eyes searching the darkness for any movement, but all was still. He pulled to a halt at the back of the hotel, secured his horse and opened the back door carefully. There was no one in the dimly lit corridor and Frank moved swiftly to the curtain across the archway at the other end. He peered round the edge of the curtain into the lobby of the hotel. The sole occupant was the clerk who dozed behind the reception desk. Frank crept stealthily forward and walked quietly up the stairs.

Once in the upstairs corridor he hurried to room seven and tapped lightly on the door.

'Come in.' Frank answered the feminine voice by opening the door and, stepping inside, closed the door quickly behind him.

'Frank!' Surprise showed both in her voice and on her face when Rose Fulton saw her visitor. 'It's a long time since I've had the pleasure. What brings you here?'

'I need your help, Rose,' answered Frank.

'I am only too pleased to help you in any way I can, Frank, you know that,' smiled Rose. 'After all you did for me five years ago I will never be out of your debt.' She indicated a chair to the rancher and, as she poured out two drinks, Frank watched her. He saw a pretty, oval-faced girl of about twenty-five whose dark hair was piled high on her head. She held herself erect and her black full-length dress fitted tightly, accentuating her curvaceous figure. Although she worked at the Ace of Spades as a singer Rose Fulton was liked and respected in Santa Rosa. There was something about her which kept her apart from the other saloon girls.

'Well, Frank?' she said as she sat down.

'Somebody is trying to frame me,' explained Frank and went on to tell Rose of the recent happenings. 'Wheeler and Farrell

147

are good friends,' he went on, 'I was wondering if you could git any information for me? I think Wheeler is sweet on you.'

Rose smiled. 'He is,' she said, 'but I prefer to keep him at arm's length. However, for you I'll play him along.'

'Thanks,' said Frank. 'Can I ask you one more favour?'

'Name it,' replied Rose.

'I can't be seen around town an' I need somewhere to stay if necessary,' explained Frank.

'Stay right here,' answered Rose without hesitation. 'Use my adjoining room as if it were yours.'

'I'm very grateful to you, Rose,' said Frank.

With the aid of Rose, Frank left the hotel unseen. He hurried quickly along the back street until he reached the end of the town where he crossed the main street without being seen. Frank moved unerringly through back streets and alleys until he was outside the bank. The building was in darkness, and, knowing he dare not venture on to the main street, Frank quickly examined both sides and the back of the building. All the windows were barred so he turned his attention to the rear door. Persistent work on the lock forced it open and Frank hurried through the bank to Grove Farrell's office. The door was unlocked and Frank started to work through Farrell's desk examining the papers by the light of the moon.

He had been there about ten minutes without finding anything of help when he was startled by the scraping of a key in the front door. Frank turned to the door of the office but before he reached it he realised he was too late; he was trapped! In three strides he was beside a tall chest of drawers behind which he crouched, hoping that whoever entered the office would not light a lamp.

The office door opened and Frank saw a man enter, leaving the door ajar, and cross to the desk. The young rancher tensed himself as a match scraped, flared and momentarily dimmed as it was applied to the wick of a lamp. Replacing the glass chimney, the man turned up the light and Frank saw that the new arrival was the bank manager. Realising it would only be a matter of moments before he was discovered, Frank eased his Colt from its holster and stood up.

Farrell's eyes widened with surprise and shock when Frank revealed himself.

'McCoy!' he gasped.

'Good evenin',' drawled Frank. 'Jest sit down an' keep your hands on the desk.'

The bank manager did as he was told and as he sat down he stared curiously at Frank. 'How did you get in here and what you want?' he asked.

'Sorry I damaged your back door,' apologised Frank with a smile. 'Now as regards what I want here I guess a talk with you will serve the purpose.'

'I haven't time to sit here talking,' hissed Farrell. 'I'll hev you arrested for illegal entry.'

'You'll make time,' snapped Frank who suddenly decided to try to bluff Farrell into giving information away. 'An' after you've heard what I know about you you'll not dare to go to the sheriff.'

Frank detected a flash of fear in the man's eyes but he quickly controlled himself. 'You've got nothing on me,' said Farrell with a hollow laugh.

'Then jest sit back an' listen,' said Frank, deciding that some of his theories might hit the mark. 'Somebody wants to run this territory,' he went on, watching Farrell carefully. 'Acting through you they bought up all available land and then they wanted the ranches. We wouldn't sell so they are trying to force us out.' In spite of his effort to control himself Farrell was so surprised by Frank's words that he glanced nervously at the man with the

150

gun. Frank noted this reaction and pressed his point. 'You're in this deep, Farrell, men hev been killed fer this land an' thet's murder. Anybody passing information to enable these raids to be carried out is jest as guilty. You…'

'Wait a minute, McCoy,' cut in Farrell. He hesitated, licked his dry lips and with a frightened look in his eyes watched Frank nervously. 'I suppose you want to know who's behind this.'

'Sure,' answered Frank, 'an' you to stand up in court an' testify.'

Farrell's brain pounded. Here was a chance to get even with MacCarthy; to teach him that Grove Farrell was not a man to blackmail nor threaten. 'If I give you this information, McCoy,' said the bank manager, 'can you guarantee thet my indiscretions will be overlooked.'

'Wal, I…'

Frank's words were drowned by the roar of a Colt. Farrell's eyes widened with surprise; his mouth dropped open and he slumped forward on to the desk. Frank, who was momentarily shocked by the unexpected explosion, spun round as the door slammed. He leaped forward, flung open the door and fired his Colt. But he was too late, the outer door was already swinging shut. Feet pounded up the sidewalk as Frank ran to the door. He was outside in a flash but already the killer had vanished up an alley. People were running towards the bank. Frank hesitated. A Colt roared and a bullet shattered the woodwork close to his head. Frank looked round desperately then suddenly turned back into the bank. He ran to the back door, and as he ran down the street he heard the shouts when the body was discovered. McCoy moved quickly from one alley and street to another and although the townsfolk searched for the killer he managed to avoid coming close to them.

He reached the end of the town when the search was at its height and realised it was highly probable that he would be seen if he attempted to cross the main street to make his way back to the hotel. Somehow or other he must make the searchers think he had left town. A horse was tied to the railings of the third house along Main Street, and Frank stepped on to the road and hurried towards the animal. He had almost reached it when a man left the house and walked down the path towards the gate. Frank broke into a run tugging his Colt from its holster as he did so. As Frank unhitched the horse, the unarmed man rushed through the gateway only to stop short in his tracks as McCoy menaced him with the Colt. Frank swung into the saddle and kicked the horse into a gallop away from town. Immediately the man started yelling, and it was not long before Frank heard the sounds of pursuit. Clouds scudded across the moon, periodically blanketing the country-side in darkness. Frank watched the sky anxiously, thankful that the cloud was thickening. About two miles out of town, Frank seized the opportunity presented by one of the periods of darkness, and turned off the trail to a group of low hillocks. He drew rein, listening intently and smiled to himself when he heard the hooves of the pursuing horses thunder past along the trail.

As the pound of the hooves faded into the distance Frank slipped from the saddle, slapped the horse hard on its flank sending it galloping further into the hills, and then set off to walk back to Santa Rosa.

The town had settled down after the ex-citement and Frank made his way quickly to the hotel. Making sure there was no one about he entered the alley at the side of the hotel. Standing on a water-butt he pulled himself up on to a sloping roof which met the hotel wall just beneath the windows of the upstairs floor. He scrambled up quickly, raised the window of Rose Fulton's room and slid over the sill.

It was shortly after midnight when Frank heard Rose come in. Waiting until she had lit a lamp, he knocked on the adjoining door and opened it.

'Frank, what on earth happened to you?' asked Rose. 'You've got into it deep this time.'

Frank told her the story of his visit to the bank and the subsequent events. 'I must hev been recognised outside the bank,' he concluded, 'so I'll hev a murder charge over my head.'

'And I've been unable to find anything out so far,' added Rose gloomily.

'I'll slip out of town before dawn,' said Frank, 'an' head for Black Water Canyon. If you find anything out let Mark Stevens know.'

Chapter Ten

When Butch Lant saw Grove Farrell slump on to his desk he slammed his smoking Colt back into its holster, ran from the bank and turned into the darkness of the first alley. Hearing people running towards the bank, and estimating that he had not been seen, Butch waited until he was certain that pursuit was not forthcoming. Stepping back on to Main Street he joined the crowd for a moment before slipping away to the Ace of Spades.

Lant found MacCarthy and Wheeler in the upstairs room and quickly reported what had happened.

'Good work,' praised MacCarthy when Butch finished his story, 'You did right to stop him spilling everything to McCoy.' His thoughtful looked changed to a smile. 'That gentleman may well be in deep trouble now. Let's go down and find out what's happening.'

When the three men left the Ace of Spades they stopped the sheriff who was hurrying along the street.

'What's wrong?' asked MacCarthy innocently.

'Farrell's been murdered!' replied the sheriff.

'What!' The three men looked incredulously at the lawman.

'Frank McCoy was seen at the door,' said the sheriff. 'Seems he's our man.'

'McCoy!' Wheeler showed surprise. 'But...'

'Yeah, that's what I thought,' interrupted the sheriff. 'I can't figure out why he should do it. He's somewhere in town so if you gentlemen would like to help...'

He was interrupted by the pound of hooves and a shout from along the street.

'McCoy! McCoy! He's headin' out of town.'

A few minutes later a posse pounded in pursuit and MacCarthy, Wheeler and Lant returned to the Ace of Spades.

With their search now having a double purpose, Clint Schofield and Zeke Dolan worked their way along Black Water Canyon, unaware that their progress was being closely followed.

About mid-morning they halted close to a cut in the precipitous west wall of the canyon and started to examine the cliff-face more closely. Their shadower moved in nearer and under the protective cover of some huge boulders watched the two men carefully. The man tensed himself when he saw Zeke move into the cleft. Five minutes later Zeke reappeared, shouting at the top of his voice.

'Clint! Clint! We've done it!' His eyes blazed with excitement; his body trembled as he held out his hands.

Clint gasped when he saw the two huge gold nuggets resting on the palms of Zeke's hands. He stared, wide-eyed at them for a few moments then suddenly let out a great whoop, threw his hat high into the air, and slapped Zeke on the back.

'Where did you find it?' he asked eagerly.

'Thet cleft runs back into the cliff. I don't know how far but a few yards inside the cleft there's a small cave. I found them there. Looks as if there might be a vein. We should be...'

His words were cut short by the crash of a rifle. Zeke jerked backwards as the bullet crashed into his chest, his knees buckled, his arms dropped by his side and the nuggets fell on to the rocky ground. Zeke pitched to the ground and lay still. Clint was momentarily frozen to the spot by the shock of seeing sudden death come to his friend, then, galvanised into action, he dived for cover as a bullet sprayed the rock above his head. He pulled his Colt from its holster but before he could position himself for firing he heard the sound of hooves along the canyon.

As Frank McCoy rode into view Bob Hart raised his rifle but, recognising McCoy from the description given to him by MacCarthy, and, remembering MacCarthy's instructions that McCoy should not be killed, he held his fire. Bob Hart cursed his luck, if only he had killed the other prospector as well he would have been the only one to know there was gold in Black Water Canyon. Instead he had to be content to slip away unobserved.

Peering cautiously round the rock Clint was relieved to see Frank. Realising his attacker must have gone, he stood up and called to his friend.

'What happened?' asked Frank, startled by the sight of the body.

'Someone shot at us,' replied Clint. 'Reckon if you hadn't shown up he'd hev made sure of me. He must hev been trailin' us an' when he saw Zeke had discovered gold thought he'd hev it fer himself.'

'Gold!' Frank gasped, hardly able to

158

believe his friend.

'Shore, right over there,' said Clint pointing at the cleft.

'But if he wanted the gold fer himself why didn't he take a shot at me?' puzzled Frank.

The sound of stones tumbling down the cliff face interrupted the conversation. Both men searched the wall of rock with their eyes but did not see any movement.

'I reckon we'll hev a look around,' said Frank, 'maybe we'd better start up there.'

Half an hour later the two men were near the top of the cliff face. Frank moved cautiously up the last few feet and peered over the edge of the cliff. There was no one in sight so he pulled himself over the edge of the cliff and turned to help Clint up the last few feet.

Once they had recovered their breath the two men searched for some trace of the killer but with no immediate success. Half a mile from the edge of the canyon they were about to give up the search when Frank grasped Clint's arm.

'Listen,' he whispered.

The two men inclined their heads listening intently as the low murmur of voices drifted to them on the faint breeze. Frank and Clint moved stealthily forward until they realised that the voices came from a hollow a short distance ahead. Creeping forward they positioned themselves so that they could see into the hollow from the cover of some rocks. Four men lounged around a fire and everything indicated that the hollow had been used as a camp for some time. The two friends watched the scene for a few minutes and then Clint tapped Frank on the arm and with a nod of his head indicated that they should move away. When they reached a safe distance from the hollow Clint stopped.

'Reckon we've found the rustlers,' said Frank.

'Know who they are?' asked Clint. Frank shook his head. 'I recognised some of the Hart gang,' replied the older man.

'From Colorado?' gasped Frank incredulously.

'Yes,' answered Clint. 'When Zeke an' I were coming up here we heard they'd been badly shot up in some raid.'

'Maybe whoever is behind this land buyin' has hired them to raid the ranchers,' said Frank thoughtfully.

'Looks like it,' agreed Clint. 'Bob Hart wasn't with them; he could be Zeke's killer.'

'But why isn't he with the others?' said Frank.

'I've been doing some hard thinkin',' replied Clint. 'Zeke was killed fer one of two reasons, either because of the gold or maybe he'd discovered unknowingly the where-abouts of the stolen cattle. I remember he remarked about the cleft going right back into the cliff, he hadn't explored it all when he found the gold. Maybe it could lead us to the steers.'

'It's a chance worth trying later,' agreed Frank.

'I reckon Bob Hart is headin' fer town to report this matter to whoever's hired him,' went on Clint.

'Then thet's where we'll head fer,' said Frank. 'You go straight to town, Clint, an' tell the sheriff about this gang; tell him I'll warn the ranchers and we'll meet him two miles south of town.'

The two men made their way back to their horses and were soon heading out of Black Water Canyon.

Pulling his Stetson further over his face and turning up the collar of his shirt Bob Hart rode slowly up Main Street of Santa Rosa so as not to attract attention. Although he did not know where to find Eugene MacCarthy he did know that the bank manager was part of the setup so, with head bent, he looked for the bank. Pulling up outside the building he strolled inside and, finding three customers at the counter, he crossed to the door marked 'Manager'. He knocked lightly and stepped quickly inside, shutting the door behind him. Hart was so surprised to see MacCarthy sitting behind the desk that he was speechless.

'Hart! What are you doing here?' Annoyance surged in MacCarthy's voice. 'I told you it would be dangerous for you to come to town.'

'I wouldn't be here if it wasn't important,' rapped Hart recovering from his surprise. 'I was keeping tag on two prospectors, who appeared to know McCoy; one of them entered the cleft to the valley where we hev the cattle. Whether he found where the cleft went I don't know but he reappeared holding gold nuggets.'

'What!' MacCarthy sat upright, his eyes widening with astonishment. He stared unseeingly in front of him. 'Gold!' he whispered. 'This is better than I thought.' Suddenly he jerked back to reality. 'You eliminated them both I hope?' he asked.

'I got one of them,' answered Hart, 'an' was goin' to deal with the other when

McCoy turned up. I could hev shot him but your instructions ruled thet out.'

'Quite right,' said MacCarthy. 'We'll be able to deal with them when we like. You left one of your outfit to watch them?'

Bob looked downcast. 'No,' he said quietly. 'I rode straight here with the news, must hev been the excitement at seeing the gold...'

'Fool!' snapped MacCarthy banging his fist on the desk. 'Now, we've lost touch with them.' He glared angrily at the outlaw. 'Things are going well. Farrell was selling us out and had to be eliminated; McCoy was blamed for the killing so we must get tags on him again quickly.' He paused, looking hard at the outlaw. 'I don't want any slip-ups now.' His voice was quiet but full of meaning.

Any further conversation was interrupted by a knock on the door.

'Come in,' shouted MacCarthy thinking it would be one of the clerks. Both men were taken aback when the sheriff entered the room.

'Sorry to bother you, MacCarthy,' he started. 'I wanted to...' he stopped; a look of amazement crossed his face. 'Bob Hart!' He gasped and his hand flew towards his holster. Like a flash of lightning Hart's gun appeared in his hand.

'Hold it, lawman,' he rapped.

The sheriff's hand froze to the butt of his Colt. He looked from one man to the other. 'What's all this about?' he asked.

'Sorry for the reception,' apologised Mac-Carthy with a grin.

He moved to the sheriff, withdrew the Colt from its holster, removed the bullets from the chamber and dropped the weapon back into the leather. 'Now nobody will suspect that anything is wrong when we escort you to your jail to end your term of office.'

The sheriff was so surprised at what was happening he could not speak.

'This was bound to happen,' continued MacCarthy, 'but your coming here has just moved things a bit quicker. I'm taking over this town, in fact the whole territory; I'm the man behind all this land buying and these raids, but McCoy is getting the blame for the lot.' He motioned towards the door. 'Let's go,' he said, 'but don't try anything, Hart's hand will be close to his gun.'

The three men crossed the street to the sheriff's office and the lawman was soon locked in one of the cells.

'Wait here, Bob,' instructed MacCarthy, 'I'll get Wheeler to put a man in here then we can deal with McCoy and his old friend.'

He started towards the door but before he reached it Clint Schofield burst in.

'Where's the sheriff?' he asked. 'I've seen the Hart gang in the mountains, and we...' he stopped when he saw the muzzle of a Colt pointing at him. He stared for a moment at the man who was holding it. 'Bob Hart!' His voice was scarcely above a whisper.

Bob grinned. 'This is one of the prospectors I told you about, Mister MacCarthy,' he said. 'Lucky fer you McCoy arrived,' he added addressing Clint.

'You shot Zeke!' Clint's eyes narrowed hatefully.

'Things seem to be playing into our hands,' smiled MacCarthy. 'Put him in a cell next to the sheriff.'

Whilst Bob Hart escorted Clint to the cells MacCarthy hurried to the Ace of Spades to return a few minutes later with one of Wheeler's men.

'Don't let anyone contact the prisoners,' instructed MacCarthy. 'Bob, this thing's slap bang in the open now, I reckon you'd better ride out to Black Water Canyon and bring your men into town.'

As Bob Hart rode out of Santa Rosa Eugene MacCarthy returned to the Ace of Spades.

Chapter Eleven

'Why do you keep putting me off when I ask you to marry me?' Floyd Wheeler watched Rose Fulton closely as she half turned from him. She looked down at her hands before answering. Rose realised if she played things correctly she might get some information which would be of use to Frank McCoy.

'Floyd, you know I've been used to better times and although people here are kind to me this isn't the kind of life I want.' Rose Fulton's voice was quiet but serious. 'If I married you then it would always be the Ace of Spades.'

'It needn't be, Rose,' replied Wheeler. There was something in the tone of his voice which indicated to Rose that there was more to tell.

Rose looked at Floyd. 'What do you mean? This is your place and your life,' she said.

'It's not always going to be like this,' said Wheeler earnestly. 'There are better times coming. I'll come into a sizeable amount of cash and will be able to pick out my own piece of land before very long.' Wheeler warmed to his subject and as he continued Rose came close to him, slipping her arm through his and her eyes shone with excitement keeping him interested in his topic. 'As a matter of fact I've already picked it out. There's a pretty creek on McCoy's spread; wooded slopes, a wonderful place to build a house. I'll build you one there and you and I...'

'But Frank McCoy will never sell,' cut in Rose. 'He's buying land, not selling.'

'Marry me, Rose, and it will be all yours,' said Wheeler.

'But how...?' Rose looked surprised. 'I don't understand. If I thought you could...'

'Of course I can,' replied Floyd. 'There are big changes going to take place around here and when they do Floyd Wheeler will be right there with them. I'll be a man of importance around here and Mrs Floyd Wheeler will be looked up to.' Rose looked questioningly at him. 'Don't ask too many questions,' continued Wheeler, 'but with a new man around here McCoy's finished and I'm backing the new man.'

'New man? What do you mean?' Rose looked puzzled.

Floyd smiled and drew the girl towards

him. 'I told you not to be inquisitive,' said Floyd. He kissed her and as their lips parted there was a tap on the door and Eugene MacCarthy walked in.

'Sorry, if I'm interrupting,' apologised MacCarthy when he saw Rose slip out of Wheeler's arms.

'That's all right,' said Rose. 'I was just going.' Her thoughts raced – could Mac-Carthy be the new man? When she reached the door she stopped, turned and played a hunch. 'You can be the first to congratulate us,' she said. 'Floyd has persuaded me to marry him.'

'Good, congratulations,' smiled Mac-Carthy.

'He tells me there's a new man going to be boss around here,' said Rose, 'Floyd will have plenty of money and a nice place to build a house; and that's what I want.'

MacCarthy flashed an angry glance at Wheeler and, although he regained his composure almost immediately, the look did not go unnoticed by Rose. Her brain pounded – had she surmised correctly? She was hardly aware that MacCarthy was speaking.

'That will be nice for you and I hope whatever transactions are carried out will be through my bank,' he said.

'I'm sure they will,' replied Rose. 'Goodbye.' She left the room but after shutting the door waited. She glanced along the balcony and seeing no one about turned towards the door listening intently.

'You fool!' She heard MacCarthy's voice raised in anger. 'How much have you opened your big mouth?'

'I've said nothing,' protested Wheeler.

'Then how did she know that I was taking over?' snapped MacCarthy.

'Now, hold on,' barked Wheeler. 'I want to marry that girl so I told her better times were coming and I would be able to leave the Ace of Spades. I mentioned a new man but not your name. From what I said she can't connect you with anything.'

'Maybe, but that girl could put two and two together,' pointed out MacCarthy. 'We agreed that we should say nothing until it was obvious I was running things.'

'Rose will be all right,' said Wheeler. 'Do you think she'd jeopardise the chance of gaining wealth and security with me?'

'I'm not so sure,' replied MacCarthy. 'I've found it best to trust no one. Careless talk can ruin things, so watch it in future; I don't want to see you go the same way as Farrell.' He stared coldly at Wheeler.

169

'What!' gasped Wheeler, his eyes smouldering with anger. 'Why you...'

'I'm playing for big stakes,' cut in MacCarthy, 'and I can't afford to take any chances.' His tone eased. 'Now, forget it; things are beginning to move, we've got the sheriff and one of the prospectors in jail! I've put one of your men as temporary sheriff to watch them.'

'What on earth...' Wheeler gasped incredulously.

'Things have come into the open rather suddenly,' said MacCarthy who went on to explain what had happened.

When MacCarthy finished his story Rose realised she had all the information Frank wanted so she hurried out of the Ace of Spades.

A few minutes later MacCarthy left Wheeler's room, paused at the balcony rail to glance at the people in the saloon. When he strolled down to the ground floor he stopped beside Butch Lant who was leaning on the bar.

'Have you seen Rose Fulton?' he asked.

'Yeah,' drawled Lant. 'I noticed her leave by the door at the end of the balcony.'

'I wonder why she used that door,' mused MacCarthy. He paused thoughtfully. 'I'll play this safe,' he said suddenly. 'Get on her trail, Butch, she may know too much.'

Lant drained his whiskey and hurried from the Ace of Spades. He paused on the sidewalk but there was no sign of Rose Fulton on Main Street. He started towards the hotel but stopped to lean on the sidewalk rail when he saw the girl, dressed in riding attire, emerge from the hotel. Rose hurried to the livery stables, hired a horse, and rode out of town. Butch hurried to his horse, climbed into the saddle and turned the animal in pursuit of the singer from the Ace of Spades.

Rose handled her horse skilfully, keeping it at a fast gallop until she reached the Swinging L where her furious knocking brought Gloria Stevens hurrying to the door.

'I must see Mark,' she panted. 'It's urgent!' The tone of her voice alarmed Gloria who took her quickly into a room where Mark was studying some papers. He looked up when the two ladies entered the room and an excited look, at the anticipation of vital news, came into his eyes.

'Frank told me to contact you if I got any information for him,' said Rose.

Mark looked at her eagerly. 'I know,' he said, 'What hev you found out?'

Rose was relieved when she realised that Mark would need no persuasion that her story was true. 'MacCarthy is the man behind everything,' she went on quickly. 'He bought up the land around here, organised raids by the Hart gang to force the ranchers out.'

'The Hart gang?' Mark looked puzzled.

'Yes,' replied Rose. 'Seems they're up in the mountains. MacCarthy was behind the killing of Farrell and has made things black for Frank.'

'I must get hold of Frank at once,' said Mark jumping to his feet. 'You'd better stay here with Gloria.'

'That isn't quite everything,' said Rose. 'He's sent for the Hart gang to come into town and he's got...'

Her words were lost in the roar of a Colt. An incredulous look crossed her face, she swayed and would have fallen if Mark had not jumped forward and grabbed her. She went limp in his arms and he laid her quickly but gently on the couch.

'Look after her, Gloria,' he yelled and, with Colt in hand, raced from the house. A rider was galloping away and Mark fired after him but already the range was too great.

Mark hurried back into the house. 'It was

Butch Lant,' he said. 'I'm goin' after him.'

'Be careful, Mark,' shouted Gloria anxiously, as her husband ran from the room. He unhitched his horse from the rail, leaped into the saddle and pounded in fast pursuit of Lant. The ground flashed under flying hooves but, although he kept the killer in sight, Mark gained only a little on him. He was somewhat surprised when he realised they were heading for Santa Rosa but stuck grimly to the pursuit.

'The sheriff'll deal with you,' mused Mark, 'even if you try to git MacCarthy's protection.'

When Mark thundered into Main Street there was no sign of Butch Lant so he brought his horse to a sliding halt outside the sheriff's office and was out of the saddle almost before the horse had stopped. He crossed the sidewalk in two strides, flung open the door of the office and burst into the room only to come to a sudden halt when he saw the occupants. He stared disbelievingly at them.

MacCarthy smiled from behind the desk. 'Hello, Stevens; mighty nice of you to call on us,' he grinned.

'Why you...' Mark started.

The smile vanished from MacCarthy's face

in a flash. A cold look came into his eyes. 'Don't try anything,' he snapped. 'These two men have twitching fingers, especially Lant.' He turned to the man who wore the sheriff's badge. 'Put him in the cells with the others,' he ordered, 'then Butch and I will pay a visit to Wheeler.'

Mark was escorted to the cells where he got a surprise when he saw Clint and the sheriff behind bars.

When the man had returned to the office Clint, Mark and the sheriff quickly exchanged experiences. 'Frank seems to be our only hope,' said Mark dejectedly, 'an' things are stacked against him.'

On reaching the Ace of Spades MacCarthy and Lant hurried straight to Wheeler's room. Wheeler smiled when the two men came in but the smile quickly disappeared when he saw the two grim faces before him.

'You nearly messed everything up,' snapped MacCarthy. Wheeler, who was sitting behind his desk, stared at Mac-Carthy. 'Rose Fulton was pumping you for information. She rode straight to Stevens' ranch; how much she told him before Butch got there I don't know but things could be pretty awkward for us.'

The realisation of Rose Fulton's fate

suddenly shocked Wheeler. As he rose to his feet his hand closed over a gun lying in an open drawer.

'You murdering...' hissed Wheeler, his voice scarcely above a whisper. He jerked the weapon upwards, but the movement had been noticed by Lant and his Colt was already in his hand. Before Wheeler could fire, Lant squeezed the trigger and a roar filled the room. Wheeler grasped at his stomach, doubled up and pitched forward on to the desk. MacCarthy stared at the body for a moment then calmly went to the door and called to two men in the saloon to remove the body.

As the door closed MacCarthy sat down behind the desk.

'Guess we may as well make use of this place,' he said. He looked thoughtful for a moment. 'Butch, I reckon we had better not take any risks; send a man to kill Mrs Stevens. She may know as much as her husband.'

Chapter Twelve

When Frank McCoy left Clint Schofield he rode hard for the Lazy A and, although he knew Abe Carson's man was watching the ranch, he rode in openly.

'You shouldn't have ridden in like that,' said Abbe anxiously after she had greeted her husband. 'Didn't Clint and Zeke contact you and tell you the ranch was being watched?'

'Yes,' replied Frank, 'but don't worry, I wanted Abe Carson's man to see me.' He went on to tell his story quickly.

'But what are you goin' to do now?' asked Abbe anxiously when her husband had finished.

'Clint's gone to warn the sheriff and I'm goin' to warn the ranchers; we'll meet the sheriff and flush this gang out, that may force whoever is behind it all into the open.'

There was a loud knocking at the front door. Abbe looked anxiously at Frank. 'Thet'll be Abe Carson's man, let's see him.' When they opened the door they found themselves covered by a Colt.

'I'm sorry, Frank,' apologised the cowboy. 'My orders were to take you into town if you showed up here.'

'I know,' answered Frank, 'but a lot has happened since that order was given.' Frank explained the latest developments but the man was not convinced and it was not until nearly an hour later that he agreed to give Frank a chance.

'Ride to Abe and your neighbours and tell them to meet the sheriff two miles south of town,' instructed Frank and as the man rode away Frank turned to Abbe. 'I'm not takin' any of our men in case someone tries to get at me through you.' They walked out of the house and a few moments later Frank was heading for the Swinging L at a fast gallop.

Gloria Stevens hurried on to the verandah when she heard the sound of a galloping horse and was relieved to see that the rider was Frank McCoy.

'I'm so glad you're here, Frank,' greeted Gloria as Frank pulled up outside the ranch-house. He detected the worried note in her voice and the troubled look in her eyes. 'Mark's in terrible danger; I was just going to ride for Tay to send him after Mark.'

'What's happened?' asked Frank as they

went into the house. He received a shock when Gloria told him of Rose Fulton's murder. 'After Mark had gone after Lant, Rose told me that MacCarthy's started to take over the town, he's already got the sheriff and Clint Schofield in jail. With MacCarthy in command Lant is sure to head back to town and Mark will ride straight into trouble.' Her eyes looked pleadingly at Frank.

'Don't worry, Gloria, I'll follow him. Send Tay to the ranchers on this side an' tell them to meet me two miles south of town.'

Suddenly Frank stiffened and as Gloria was about to speak he signalled her to be quiet. A faint creak came from outside the window. Frank turned sharply then flung himself at Gloria sending them both crashing to the floor as a Colt roared. Frank twisted to one side dragging his gun from its holster. He saw a face at the window as a man moved quickly to a position from which he could take another shot. Frank squeezed his trigger and saw the man crash backwards as the bullet hit him between the eyes. McCoy scrambled to his feet and helped Gloria from the floor.

There was a frightened look in her eyes. 'Who was it?' she asked.

'One of Lant's cronies,' replied Frank grimly. 'I guess Butch must hev reached town, an' MacCarthy, figuring that Rose may have told you everything, decided you were better dead.'

'Then Mark...' Gloria left her thoughts unspoken.

'He's probably all right,' answered Frank quickly. 'I must get going.' When they walked outside they saw two riders approaching. 'It's Tay with one of your men,' said Frank. 'Put them in the picture; tell Tay to ride fast and keep the other man here with you.'

Gloria nodded and as Frank swung into the saddle, he saw a look in her eyes which pleaded with him to hurry with his task.

He kept his horse at an earth pounding gallop but as he rounded a low hill near Santa Rosa he hauled hard on the reins bringing the animal to a sliding halt. Five men were riding steadily towards the town! The Hart gang had beaten him to it! Frank rode cautiously into town and made his way along the back streets to the rear of the sheriff's office hoping he would not be too late. He knocked loudly on the door and a few moments later he heard someone call 'Who is it?'

'I have a message from MacCarthy,' replied Frank.

'Why didn't you come to the front door?' came the cautious question.

'MacCarthy didn't want me to be seen,' answered Frank.

He heard the bolts being drawn and the key grating in the lock. With gun drawn Frank drew back against the wall to one side of the door. The door swung open and seeing no one immediately in front of him the man peered round the doorway. Frank pounced, bringing his Colt crashing down on the man's head. He pitched to the ground and Frank dragged him quickly into the building. After picking the key up from the sheriff's office McCoy hurried to the cells where the three prisoners jumped to their feet with surprise when Frank appeared.

'How did you know we were here?' asked Mark.

'Rose told Gloria about Clint and the sheriff after you'd gone,' explained Frank. 'I guessed you'd walk right into trouble when you didn't know the sheriff had been seized. One of Lant's cronies tried to kill Gloria but fortunately I was at the Swinging L.'

The sheriff gathered their guns from the office whilst Mark and Clint gagged and tied MacCarthy's man before locking him in a cell.

'Right,' said the sheriff, 'let's get Mac-Carthy.' He moved towards the door but

Frank halted him.

'We can't,' he said and went on to explain. 'The Hart gang have arrived already. I saw them ridin' in. It would be suicide for us four to attempt to get them. I sent word to all the ranchers to gather two miles south of town an' I reckon we should ride there to reinforce our numbers.'

The three men agreed and they all hurried to the back door locking it after them when they left. The sheriff hurried to the end of the building and glanced cautiously into the side street. 'Our horses hev been moved round here,' he called and soon the four men were riding cautiously through the back streets towards the edge of town. Once they were clear they pushed their mounts into a fast gallop southwards.

When they reached the pre-arranged meeting place they found the ranchers and a number of their men already gathered together questioning one another as to what it was all about. Tom Price glared at Frank as the four men pulled to a halt. 'Has McCoy got us on some wild scheme to try to throw the wool over our eyes?' shouted Price.

'Hold it, Tom,' called the sheriff. 'Frank's just busted us out of jail. MacCarthy's the man behind all the trouble, he's taken over the town and the Hart gang have ridden in to join him.'

A murmur ran through the bunch of riders. Frank explained events in more detail and when he had finished Price pushed his horse forward alongside McCoy. He held out his hand.

'I'm sorry, Frank,' he apologised.

Frank gripped his hand firmly. 'Now you can see the association in action,' he said.

With the sheriff in the lead the group of horsemen thundered towards Santa Rosa.

Eugene MacCarthy was standing on the balcony in the Ace of Spades when Bob Hart and his gang walked in. He greeted them with a wave and signalled them to come straight up to what had once been Wheeler's room. Butch Lant summoned seven men from the saloon whom he knew could be trusted to do jobs without questions being asked. Once introductions were over Mac-Carthy seated himself behind the desk, lit a cheroot and glanced round the men in front of him.

'You have chosen to ride with me, stick by me and you will be well rewarded,' he said. 'I aim to rule all the territory and you are the men who will see things are run my way; new recruits will be taken on as and when necessary but in the meantime Hart will work with his gang and Lant will lead the rest of you. Things are beginning to move fast, and, with the bank and the office of sheriff already in my hands, the citizens of Santa Rosa will soon realise the best way for peace of mind is on my side of the fence.' He paused and drew at his cheroot. 'The ranchers will soon come to heel when more pressure is brought to bear on them,' he continued. 'One other thing in our favour,' he added with a smile, 'there's gold in Black Water Canyon!'

A murmur of excitement ran through the men. 'You'll all get your fair share of that,' called out MacCarthy to quieten the noise. 'The first thing we are going to do is to show folks that our new setup as sheriff believes in action; we'll bring McCoy to justice and, with our crimes pinned on him, we'll be in the clear. Butch, bring the old prospector from the jail, we want to know where McCoy is; Bob said they were together in the canyon.'

Lant nodded and left the Ace of Spades. Ten minutes later the door burst open and Lant, followed by the guard from the sheriff's office, burst into the room.

'They've gone!' panted Lant.

'What!' MacCarthy slammed his fist on the desk and glared angrily at the two men. 'What happened?' he snapped.

'I answered a knock at the back door,' explained the guard. 'Hombre said he had a message from you. When I opened the door he jumped me.'

'Did you see who it was?' rapped Mac-Carthy.

The man shook his head. 'No,' he answered.

'Fool!' snarled MacCarthy. He looked round the men in the room. 'Those three know too much,' he said grimly. 'We've got to get them, search the town.'

The men filed quickly out of the room but half an hour later they returned in ones and twos with nothing to report.

MacCarthy looked thoughtful when the last man came in. 'I figure McCoy sprang those three out of jail. When Lant shot Rose Fulton, Stevens followed him, that left only one person who could have known we had those men in jail and that was Mrs Stevens.'

'She could hev sent some of the ranch hands,' pointed out Bob Hart.

'True,' agreed MacCarthy, 'but I reckon if there had been a bunch of them they would have ridden straight into town, but this was done much more subtly. I figure McCoy came out of Black Water Canyon sent the old prospector to town whilst he tried to contact Stevens. Lant's sidekick must have been too late to eliminate Mrs Stevens so that McCoy learned what had happened from her so he came to town and got them out of jail.'

'What do we do now, boss?' asked Lant.

'The whole story will soon be in the hands of the ranchers,' replied MacCarthy, 'so I figure we'll try to take one more trump card – Mrs McCoy.'

MacCarthy rose to his feet and, followed by his band of gunmen, hurried from the Ace of Spades. They swung on to their horses and were turning them when the pound of hooves from the south end of the town caused MacCarthy to halt. He glanced at Bob Hart who sat calmly on his horse his hand resting on the butt of his Colt.

'Could be this is the showdown?' said Hart quietly.

'It is,' answered MacCarthy as the group of riders pounded into view.

Seeing MacCarthy's men the ranchers hauled hard on the reins bringing their mounts to a sliding halt. Men dived from their saddles as a hail of lead met them.

MacCarthy yelled instructions to his men and jumped into the doorway of the Ace of Spades. Bob Hart was beside him, throwing lead in the direction of the ranchers. Gradually the initial, all-out firing died down as both sides took stock of their position.

MacCarthy shouted to two of his men and as they leaped from the cover of a water trough he and Hart gave them covering fire. The first man flung himself into the doorway but the second man was still there yards away when a bullet spun him on to the sidewalk where he lay still.

'Get upstairs with a rifle,' MacCarthy instructed.

The man hurried away and a few moments later his accurate fire accounted for two cowboys.

The sheriff signalled to Tom Price and Abe Carson to follow him and they made their way quickly up a side-street to try to move round behind MacCarthy's men. As they turned the corner at the end of the street they came face to face with three members of the Hart gang who had had a similar idea. Lead flew and the three outlaws pitched into the dust. The sheriff glanced quickly at his two companions and leaped to Abe's side when he saw him stagger.

'It's nothing,' said Abe brushing off the sheriff's help as he steadied him. 'Only a flesh wound. Come on let's git round these hombres.'

The three men ran along the street their guns held ready for any surprise attack. When they reached the main street they took MacCarthy's gang by surprise and, caught between two fires, several men threw down their guns and raised their arms.

'It's all up,' said Bob Hart grimly.

'For us it's not,' answered MacCarthy. 'Come on we'll go through the Ace of Spades.' The two men squeezed through the half open door carefully in case any movement should give their position away but their escape attempt had not gone unnoticed. Butch Lant from a doorway a little further along the block saw them go. He hesitated, glanced round and, seizing the right opportunity jumped from his cover and, in a crouching run, sprinted for the doorway. He had almost covered the distance before bullets spanged around him but somehow he reached the Ace of Spades unharmed.

'Reckon MacCarthy's in the Ace of Spades,' Frank said turning to Mark, 'an' if so he can escape through the door from the balcony.'

'Let's git round there,' said Mark who raised himself cautiously from the cover of some barrels only to be sent diving back as the rifle spoke from an upstairs room in the Ace of Spades.

'We're pinned down here,' called Frank. 'MacCarthy will…'

His words were halted as a rifle cracked from the room above them. He saw a rifle drop from the window of the Ace of Spades and a man fall forward across the window-frame. Frank looked at Mark in surprise and was even more astonished when Clint dropped from the roof above them.

'Reckoned the only way to git thet hombre was to git on level terms with him,' panted Clint with a smile, 'an' I got him lined up whilst he was given his attention to you.'

'Thanks,' said Frank. 'Now cover us.' He leaped to his feet and, followed by Mark, raced across the street. Clint's rifle kept up a withering fire and the two men reached the cover of a building without mishap. They hurried forward moving round the Ace of Spades towards the exit from the balcony. As they rounded the corner they saw the door being opened slowly and they jumped back into cover. They tensed themselves and waited until they heard the footsteps on the wooden stairs. Suddenly they stepped round the corner.

'Hold it, MacCarthy,' yelled Frank.

MacCarthy and Hart froze on the stairs. Hart's gun was up in a flash but as his finger squeezed the trigger Mark's bullet crashed into his chest. He staggered, toppled against the rail, slipped and rolled past MacCarthy to the bottom of the steps. MacCarthy stood petrified as the two men advanced slowly towards him. Their attention was so riveted on MacCarthy that they did not react immediately Butch Lant appeared. The killer's Colt roared and Mark felt a searing pain in his arm. He staggered sideways but Frank's Colt sent lead crashing into Lant whose knees buckled throwing him into a silent heap.

The whine of bullets around him seemed to drive life into MacCarthy. He leaped forward and at the same time jerked a gun from a holster. He fired but Frank was that fraction quicker. He dived to one side firing as he did so. MacCarthy stopped in his tracks, his hands grasping at his stomach, his eyes widened and he pitched forward face downwards in the dust.

Frank got to his feet, and glanced at the silent forms which marked the end of Eugene MacCarthy's attempt to take over the territory. Mark's wound wasn't serious and when the two friends rejoined the sheriff and the ranchers Frank asked them to be at the Lazy A at eleven o'clock the following morning.

When all the men had gathered at the Lazy A Frank informed them that he and Clint had been in the saddle early and Clint's theory regarding the whereabouts of the stolen cattle had proved correct.

'This means,' he went on, 'that once things are fixed up at the bank, Sheridan and Price can be back in the cattle business.' An excited murmur broke out but Frank called for silence. 'There's one further point,' he said. 'Clint and his partner discovered gold in Black Water Canyon and I figure, and Abbe and Clint have agreed, that your association should become a company to run the gold mine. In this way you will all get a share, be able to pay off the debts on your ranches and purchase more land if you want it. Then we will be powerful enough to keep out any more Eugene MacCarthys.'

The ranchers jumped to their feet with excitement applauding Frank's generosity.

Clint smiled. 'Wal,' he said to Frank, 'I reckon when I git back to Red Springs I can tell Dan that his young brother is a credit to him.'

The publishers hope that this book has given you enjoyable reading. Large Print Books are especially designed to be as easy to see and hold as possible. If you wish a complete list of our books please ask at your local library or write directly to:

Dales Large Print Books
Magna House, Long Preston,
Skipton, North Yorkshire.
BD23 4ND